No Gouda Without You

A Marley Creek Romance

Victoria Hamel

PB & A Publishing

This book is dedicated to all of us, the cancer survivors. Thank you for trusting me to tell a love story about a girl who is trying to navigate survivorship.

Contents

Chapter One

Nicole Garrett flopped down across from her best friend Devin and took a big drink from the glass of water on the table.

"Labor Day is over; why is it still so hot outside?" She groused.

Devin shrugged and said, "About time you got here. I've been waiting for ten minutes. I'm dying to try the buffet. They have three different kinds of French toast, and I'm going to try all three."

Nicole smiled, "Sometimes I forget that being on time is late to you."

"You don't get to be mayor by showing up on time. You have to be prepared and five minutes early." Devin hit the table with her hand.

"But if you're a man, you can be late and take bribes," Nicole said, speaking about the ex-mayor of Marley Creek, who was now also an ex-con.

"Exactly," Devin said as she stood up. "Now let's go try this food. Sally was here last week, and she said the French toast was the best she'd ever had. And that lady knows her food."

Nicole slid back out of the booth and said, "I'm going to check out the omelet station."

Devin paused, "Please tell me you're not doing keto."

Nicole half-smiled and walked away. She crossed the restaurant. Looking into a series of mirrors lining the way, she realized she should have put the prosthetic padding into her bra. Her top was more fitted than she usually wore, and it was glaringly obvious to her that she looked lopsided. She should have worn a hoodie, but it was so hot outside that she'd left it at home. She tugged at her shirt, trying to stretch it while she hunched her shoulders.

The line for an omelet snaked around several tables and past the brick fireplace that anchored the far side of Jesse's Pub. Nicole frowned as she realized she'd left her phone back at the table. She crossed her arms to hide her chest. She looked around the pub. Even though she only lived a block away, she hadn't been here since it had reopened a couple of summers ago. Her stomach roiled as she remembered that was when she'd been in the midst of breast cancer treatment.

She absently twirled a lock of her wavy, auburn, shoulder-length bob. When Jesse's Pub had opened, she'd been avoiding most anything with flavor, opting for a diet consisting of saltine crackers, applesauce, and chicken rice soup. "That's not today, though," she mumbled to herself as she counted the people in front of her, all of whom were on their phones. She looked up at the restaurant ceiling; she didn't remember the wooden beams and the exposed brick on the walls. The pub now had a rustic farm-to- table vibe going on, which she had to admit was a nice addition to downtown Marley Creek.

Finally, it was Nicole's turn. By now, her mouth was watering. She stared down at the toppings, trying to decide what to get. On one hand, she'd love a Denver omelet smothered in cheese with a side of bacon, but on the other hand, it was so much healthier to get an egg white omelet with spinach, tomato, and mushrooms—hold the cheese and no side of bacon. Processed food was something she avoided as much as possible in her post-cancer life, even though she missed it and her oncologist said it was okay in moderation. Still, she didn t like to risk it. Her stomach growled, making her decision more difficult. A deep male voice said, "What would you like in your omelet?"

Nicole looked up into a face so handsome she completely forgot about complex carbs. "Ah," she said, her mouth agape, "What?"

He smiled and she almost gasped when dimples popped out under his two-day scruff. "What would you like in your omelet?" He waved a couple of eggs toward the variety of toppings and then cracked them into his stainless steel pan.

"Nooo," Nicole said loudly.

"I'm sorry?" The chef said, smiling.

Nicole gulped, noticing the name Sean embroidered on his chef jacket and marveling at his broad chest. She shook her head a little, trying to clear her sudden lusty thoughts. "It's just that I wanted an egg white omelet with mushrooms, spinach, and tomatoes," she blurted and felt heat rising on her neck.

"No worries." Sean smiled, dumped out the eggs, grabbed another pan, and added egg white mix to it. Nicole watched him work and hoped the floor would swallow her up. She should have gotten in the buffet line and served herself, but no, she wanted a super healthy omelet instead. Sean added the vegetables and then looked at Nicole. "What kind of cheese would you like? We've got cheddar and Swiss, and today we have a new smoked gouda from Wisconsin. Would you like a sample?" He picked up a toothpick with a chunk of cheese and held it out to Nicole.

"Oh, no thank you," Nicole said. For reasons she didn't want to understand, she couldn't even make eye contact with Sean and instead found herself staring at his full lips.

"Are you sure? It's got a nice nutty flavor. It's been a huge hit today."

"No, thank you," she repeated.

"Alright," he said, plating the egg white omelet and handing it to Nicole. Nicole grabbed the plate, her hand brushed his, and she jerked back and spun away startled, only to have her omelet fly off the plate and plop on the floor.

Her shoulders drooped, and her face burned with embarrassment. She wanted to run out of the restaurant. Nicole bent down to pick up her omelet, but before she could get it, Sean had come around with a broom and swept the omelet into a dustpan. Her eyes fixed on his Crocs, she sighed, "I should just leave."

Sean put a hand on her arm. "No one leaves my place hungry. Just stay right here and I'll have a new egg white omelet, hold the cheese, ready for you in a jiffy."

The kindness she heard in his voice helped diffuse the cloud of embarrassment hanging over her. She smiled a crooked smile, "M-maybe I should take advantage of the second chance?"

Sean quirked an eyebrow. "What did you have in mind?"

"Denver omelet, with the gouda?"

Sean gave her a dazzling smile, and she felt it all the way down to her toes. "Let's get cracking."

She groaned playfully at the pun. Sean apologized to the rest of the line and quickly made Nicole's omelet. Her mouth watered as she watched him work, mostly from the delicious smell of sauteing ham, onion, and peppers. She let her eyes slide up his chest to his neck, and then she allowed herself to take in his face. She felt a crack in her defenses when she saw the tip of his tongue stick out just a tiny bit as he flipped her omelet.

"I know you are going to love this omelet. The ham is actually from Hampshire and the green peppers are from our garden."

"You have a garden here?" She looked around as if she could see it from where she stood.

Sean plated her omelet and then held the cheese grater. "Would you like a little cheese on top?"

Nicole nodded, her auburn waves dancing around her face.

Sean once again handed her the plate. "Be careful now," he said.

"Will do," Nicole said solemnly and made her way to her table navigating the restaurant patron traffic.

Nicole slid into the booth and waved down the hostess who was refilling guests' coffee. The younger girl had long blond hair pulled up in a high ponytail and was wearing a Jesse's Pub T-shirt. Nicole felt a tiny pang of jealousy. She wished she could go back to the days when she could wear a tight T-shirt and feel good about herself. Nicole swore she knew her from somewhere but couldn't place her. Just as she was about to ask the girl her name, Devin plopped down. Her plate was heaping with French toast, strawberries, whipped cream, and a side plate of bacon. "You just got your food? I was in line for the longest time, and then my omelet fell off my plate, so I had to get a new one. I figured you'd be done eating by the time I got back to the table."

Devin paused, her fork halfway to her mouth, "You dropped your food?"

"It flew off the plate."

"Mm-hmm," Devin said, and then took a bite of her food. "Oh my god. This is so good."

Nicole took another bite of her omelet and nodded. For a few minutes, their table was silent except for the scrape of forks and a few small moans of pleasure.

"I am never not having Nutella on French toast again," Devin announced.

"This is the best breakfast I have had since I don't know when," Nicole said. As they finished their meals, Nicole asked Devin, "Why did it take you so long to get your food?"

Devin rolled her eyes. "More Oktoberfest trouble. Mrs. Woodsman," Devin gestured over her shoulder and Nicole saw the retired librarian sitting at a table next to the patio doors, "was livid. Apparently, she was out walking her dog and saw someone peeing in the alley by her house!"

"Ick."

"Yes, definitely ick, and she noticed the guy had a Hop's Heaven shirt on. Now I've got to check in with the Chief and see if we can start keeping an extra car on patrol around Hop's Heaven. Did you know that I have checked with towns all over the Midwest and we are the only one that has an Oktoberfest celebration that goes on for four weeks? All the other fests are just one or maybe two weekends in September. We aren't finished until mid-October for Pete's sake! Chief Hendrick wants to add a couple more auxiliary police officers, and Public

Works is telling me that they need to do more street sweeping and trash pickup on the surrounding streets. Do you have any idea how much overtime is costing this town?"

"No clue. That's why you're the mayor and I work at a school talking to little kids and parents all day."

"Let me tell you, it's a lot. And we're already over budget! I don't know how we are going to come up with the money or the workforce to keep up! I hate to do it, but I'm going to have to go along with Councilman Sanchez and his campaign to shut down the Oktoberfest." Devin blew out a breath in frustration. "Enough about me and my mayor woes. Did I see you hit your fifteen-year anniversary?"

"Yep, the first day of school was my anniversary!" Nicole sat up straighter.

"That's wonderful! Now you can take that dream trip to Scotland you kept talking about during your treatment. What was it you said? Cancer owes you an amazing trip because it took so much away?"

"Yeah, about that "

Devin stilled.

Nicole quickly continued, "N-nothing's wrong, I'm fine!" she waved her hands.

Devin put her hand on her heart, "You scared me there."

"I'm so sorry. I was just going to say that I've had second thoughts." She looked down at her empty plate. "I'm putting the trip on hold. I need to keep my five-year paid leave just in case, you know? What if I get sick again?"

Devin reached over and patted her hand, "Oh honey, I'm sorry you feel like that, but remember the promises you made to yourself? How beating cancer was going to be your second chance?”

Nicole frowned, “Right, that once I was done with treatment I was going to live, live, live. My bucket list wasn’t going to wait; carpe diem and all that. I remember, it’s just...I think I don’t know how to do that.”

Devin gave her hand a squeeze, “Maybe it’s time to say yes once in a while.”

Nicole pointed at her empty plate. “I say yes sometimes. Look, I even got the cheese and you know how hard I try to avoid anything processed.”

Devin laughed, “I guess I’ll have to take your word for it. That plate is *emp-ty*.”

Their laughter was interrupted by a deep voice Nicole recognized in an instant.

“Laughter and empty plates! As the owner of this fine establishment, nothing does my heart as good as seeing this.” He leaned in conspiratorially, “And a five-star review from said patrons is always appreciated.”

“We’ll see what we can do, Mister...?” Devin asked.

“Sean Harper,” he said, taking off his gloves and putting out his hand toward Devin. “Madam Mayor, you need no introduction. Thank you so much for joining us for breakfast today.”

Devin gave Sean a hearty handshake. “Wonderful to meet you, Sean. The food was fantastic!”

“You are too kind,” he put a hand to his heart.

Nicole guffawed. “Trust me, Devin isn’t one for flattery. If she says your food is fantastic, it’s fantastic.”

Sean pivoted to Nicole, his hand out, "We haven't met properly. I'm Sean, and you are?"

Nicole placed her hand in his palm. She noticed the calluses that spoke of years in the kitchen and gardening. "I'm Nicole Garrett. We're practically neighbors," she uncharacteristically gushed.

He held her hand for a moment. "It's a pleasure to meet you, Nicole." A shiver went through her as he said her name. She let go of his hand, and her cheeks reddened.

Devin interjected, "She lives one block over, around the corner from the elementary school where she works. I don't even think she owns a car."

"I do!"

"Well, I stand corrected." Devin smiled.

Nicole noticed Devin looking at Sean's hand. She knew that meant her best friend had noticed Sean didn't have any rings on. Devin must be assuming he was single and was likely planning Nicole and Sean's wedding in her mind. However, Nicole knew the lack of a ring could mean many things besides being single. Not that she was looking to date him. "We better not take up too much of your time. Thanks again for making me that second chance omelet."

Sean smiled broadly. "Speaking of chances, Nicole, would you be free to get a cup of coffee with me on Monday?"

Devin clapped her hands together, "Yes! That's a great idea!"

Nicole gave her a look; Devin folded her hands together. "You love a good latte, Nicole."

Nicole gave Devin the evil eye and turned to Sean, "That's very kind of you, but I can't make it."

Sean's face fell, and then he perked up and smiled, "Right, you work at Ida B. Wells Elementary. Okay, what about tea? After work? My treat, of course."

"Um," Nicole hesitated, "I-I'm sorry I can't."

Devin frowned but didn't say anything.

Sean chuckled nervously, "Fair enough. If you change your mind...Well, in any case, thank you so much again for coming in, Mayor Belmont." He put his hand over his heart and bowed slightly. "Please come back and bring the family."

Devin laughed, "I'll come back with Ben, but my twins? No, thank you. That's what babysitters are for!"

"Understood," Sean pivoted back to Nicole.

"Thanks again," she said, quickly getting up. "It was delicious."

"You're welcome," Sean said with a professional note in his voice and a little disappointment in his eyes. "I hope we'll run into each other again, neighbor."

Nicole smiled wanly, "It's a pretty small town." And she walked toward the door.

Chapter Two

♥

Sean watched the door swing shut behind Nicole. He ran a hand through his dark brown hair and sighed. Had he come on too strong? Maybe he'd read her wrong. He replayed their conversation in his head as he broke down the buffet. He'd loved the way the tip of Nichole's tongue had peeked out as her grin turned into a laugh. And her lips, they were just perfect for kissing. He loaded the trays and was happy to see everything from the bacon to the farmer's hash was gone. "Sean, my boy," he said to himself, "adding brunch service was a brilliant idea."

"Ahem," said a voice behind him.

Sean started and turned around, "Mable, how can I help?"

Mable, who worked as a hostess while attending graduate school, smirked, "I hope I'm not interrupting, but Charlie called off."

Sean's mouth made a straight line, all the mirth gone. "Damn it," he spat.

"I'm sorry, Mable, I shouldn't talk like that in front of you."

Mable waved a hand. "Oh, please! I've heard-heck-I've said much worse than that. Remember the time I dropped a whole tray of fresh croissants?"

"Still, I try not to swear at work, and even though you are one of my many step cousins, I try to keep it professional. You get what I'm saying, right?"

"No worries, I get it, and I'm not even sure if step cousins are a thing. Whatever the case, I consider you family. That being said, I have enough trouble keeping track of my own brothers and sisters. Do you really want to be part of my family?"

"Mable, I know how much you help your parents out with your younger siblings. Don't sell yourself short. I'm so glad you consider me family." Sean checked the time on his watch. "Well, guess I won't be able to sneak in a nap this afternoon."

"Sorry, boss but at least we don't have dinner service tonight."

"True, thank goodness we have a fixed menu for the wedding shower. Of course, when you get up at five o'clock to prep brunch, a day ending by eight instead of eleven is still pretty brutal. But you know me, is there anywhere else I'd rather be?"

"Nope," she replied and began pushing the cart of dirty pans into the kitchen, her high blonde ponytail swishing as she walked.

Sean walked over to the coffee urn and made himself a cup of coffee. If he was going to make it through the rest of the day, he was going to need all the caffeine he could get. He took his cup out to the restaurant's patio. He pulled a chair over to the large rectangle fire pit that was the centerpiece of the cobblestone patio and propped up his feet.

It was hot today, but soon temperatures would be in the fifties on a regular basis. He made a note to add creamy wild rice soup and his Grandma's chicken & dumpling soup back on the menu. Thinking of soup reminded him he needed to reach out to his best friend, Jasper Kane, owner of Hop's Heaven, Marley Creek's Craft Brewery.

Sean took out his phone and opened his contacts. He scrolled down to Jasper Kane and pressed send. Then he waited for Jasper to pick up. As the phone rang, his thoughts wandered back to Nicole. He wondered if she ever went by Nicki, and what it would feel like to wrap her up in his arms. He'd been certain she was interested in him. Maybe he was a little more drawn to her than she was to him, but darn it, he knew a flirty vibe. Why had she said no? It was just an afternoon date for coffee. No pressure. Maybe he'd run it past Jasper and get his feedback.

It had been a minute since Sean had dated someone. Starting up Jesse's Pub had been and continued to be something that consumed virtually all his waking hours. If you counted all the nightmares he had involving wrong orders, spoiled food, or coming to work without his pants on, then it would be safe to say all his time had been devoted to Jesse's over the last two years. If he was being honest with himself, he wasn't entirely sure he should date right now, but there was something about Nicole that drew him to her. Maybe dating had changed more than he knew, and he'd gone about asking Nicole out completely wrong. He didn't think so, but he might as well ask Jasper.

"Lo," Jasper answered the phone, startling Sean.

"Hey buddy, you got a minute?"

"Ya, sure. Hang on a sec."

"Am I on speakerphone?"

"Maybe? And so? It's two in the afternoon on a Sunday. We're practically empty," Jasper explained.

Sean laughed, "Dude, I don't care. No one wants to hear someone on speakerphone, and I don't want any of the gossips that hang out at your place talking about me."

"Hold on one sec."

Sean could hear a door shut.

"Okay, I'm in my office now. I can't wait to hear what's so important you don't want anyone overhearing this convo."

"I can tell I'm still on speaker," Sean pointed out.

Jasper sighed loudly. "I'm in my office. The door is shut, so no one can hear you."

"Jasper, c'mon."

"Fine. You're off speakerphone. Now my ear is going to get sweaty from holding the phone up to it. No one holds their phones up to their ears anymore, Sean."

Sean blew out air and ran a hand through his hair. "It's hard to believe that I'm the younger one in our friendship. Now, moving on, I need some advice."

"Let me guess. You met someone, but they have a kid, and that's not your thing."

"I did meet someone, and when you say it like that, it makes me sound like a jerk. I don't know if she has any kids. If she did, it wouldn't be the first time I dated someone who had one."

"Right. You did date that one girl, Bethany?" Jasper was almost sure he had the name right.

"Yes, that was her. Anyway, kids are fine. For other people."

"I get it. Although I think someday I might not mind a Jasper Jr. running around the brewery."

"I don't know if Marley Creek could handle a mini you. Now, can I tell you about what happened today?" Sean explained meeting Nicole and how she had turned him down.

"I'm telling you, Jasper, I felt a connection! I know she did too, but she turned me down."

"True, she did. She also said no when you suggested having a breakfast worth eating, right? Maybe she's someone who says no first to anything new or fun?"

Sean grinned from ear to ear. "Just when I think you're just a pretty face, you surprise me with amazing perceptiveness."

Jasper ignored the compliment. "I've got a great face and a body to match. I work out and I count all my macros. I tote kegs daily. When I pull a tap, my muscles ripple. I'm the complete package."

"Alright, alright, easy there. I was trying to thank you for the advice. Like I was saying, in addition to your ugly mug, you've got a brain hiding in there. I think you might be right. Since when have you been able to read women so well?"

"Actually," Jasper began, but Sean cut him off.

"Buddy, I've got to run and get ready for a wedding shower. Thanks for the insight. I know what I'm going to do."

"Wedding shower? Send the maid of honor my way. They're always looking for attention and I have plenty to give."

Sean laughed, "Sometimes I don't know when you're kidding or when you're serious. That's a good one, Jasp. Plenty to give."

"But I'm ser-"

Sean hung up the phone and shoved it in his back pocket. Time to get back to work, and tomorrow he could figure out how to approach Nicole.

Chapter Three

♥

Nicole poured a cup of coffee into her favorite mug and walked outside to sit on her porch so she could soak in the cloud-free fall day. She'd long held the opinion that this was the best time of year in Marley Creek. Aside from her time at college, she'd lived her whole life here, and she had no desire to live anywhere else.

Anytime she wanted to be in a world-class city, all she needed to do was hop on the train that ran through the middle of town, and in ninety minutes she'd be in downtown Chicago. Anytime she felt like a Target run, she only needed to drive twenty minutes and she'd be in a suburb surrounded by every chain store or restaurant a person could ever need.

Thanks to the commuter train, Marley Creek had avoided the sad fate of small towns all over the Midwest. Here, they'd managed to keep the small local businesses afloat in a world of online ordering because Marley Creek catered to weekenders from the city. First, it was the yuppies—with their flipped-up collars and disposable income—who came for the annual August art fair that was now celebrating its thirty-ninth year. Then, there was the annual Marley Creek Marathon that began in the year two-thousand. A few years ago, Jasper Kane opened Hop's Heaven, and Marley Creek was now part of the Illinois Craft Brewer Guild Passport Program.

Unlike most breweries, Marley Creek had built-in public transportation from anywhere in the city right to their door. Nicole had only been to Hop's Heaven a couple of times, but she appreciated how the influx of guests kept other unlikely businesses open. How many other small towns had an art gallery devoted to stained glass, two record stores, as well as a make-your-own-ramen shop? And then there was Zaina's shop, New Age Stones and Witch Crafts.

Zaina and Nicole had been friends since second grade when Scott Micos wouldn't stop calling Nicole 'Icky Nicky' and Zaina put a hex on him using a G.I. Joe. She told Scott that if he didn't leave Nicole alone, she'd break G.I. Joe's arm and Scott would feel pain every time he played baseball.

From that moment on, Zaina and Nicole had been thick as thieves. That's why on this beautiful Sunday, Nicole was going over to Zaina's shop to help her unpack her inventory order and restock the shelves for fall. In return for helping, Zaina offered Nicole free tarot card readings, but ever since she'd been diagnosed with breast cancer, the last thing Nicole wanted to know was the future. At this point, she had a dozen free tarot IOUs sitting around. That didn't matter, though. She helped Zaina because she enjoyed spending time with her best friend, and helping Zaina with her dream business always made her feel good. As Zaina frequently said, her store had good vibes.

Nicole refilled her coffee cup and poured a high-fiber, high-protein cereal into a bowl with almond milk. She ate a spoonful of the cereal, and it was so hard she was afraid she was going to break a tooth. After she tried one more bite, Nicole threw out the rest of the cereal. She rummaged in her refrigerator until she found a slightly wrinkled apple. Nicole stared at it before taking a bite and wished she was back in front of the Denver omelet Sean had made for her yesterday. "Sean," she said his name out loud to the room, seeing how it felt on her tongue. Maybe she should have agreed to meet for tea. *What could it hurt?* Her phone buzzed with a text.

Z: Ready? I'm out front!

Nicole texted back, then put her phone in her back pocket and headed out to Zaina's waiting car.

"Thanks for picking me up. You didn't have to. I could have walked."

Zaina shook her head; her platinum blonde hair was cut in a pixie which showed off the tattoo she called her protection sigil on the back of her neck. "I feel like it's going to rain. I didn't want you to get stuck in a downpour. Plus, Mike wound up leaving for his business trip last night instead of this morning, so I had nothing but extra time."

"Thanks, Z."

Nicole had always been a complete skeptic about all things witchy, but she didn't begrudge her friend her beliefs. Zania's tattoo showed a waxing crescent moon, several interlocking circles and two arrows making an X. When Nicole had been recovering from surgery, Zaina had brought her a pink candle with her sigil carved in it. Nicole was sure it was just the placebo effect, but she felt peaceful whenever she lit that candle.

Zaina pulled out onto Main Street and glanced at Nicole.

"Something is different. You look...did you meet a man?"

Nicole's mouth dropped open, "How? What? No, why? I look different?"

Zaina hit her brakes as a couple began walking into the crosswalk. She began laughing. "I'm an empath and intuitive. I'm not psychic. Devin told me about brunch."

Nicole gently face-palmed, "I'm such a dork."

Zaina tapped Nicole's knee. "You are not! But usually, you're so logical I can't put anything past you. You're also so skeptical; I'm amazed you fell for it!" She pulled into the alley behind her shop and put the car in park. "Let's go in and you can tell me all about this new man."

"Sean," Nicole corrected, "but he's not my man."

"Okay, whatever you say," Zaina said over her shoulder as she opened the door to her shop just as big plops of rain began falling from the sky. She held the door open as Nicole ran in to join her.

Nicole turned on the lights in the shop. Zaina prepared hot water and made sure the tea station was restocked for anyone who might pop in during their inventory restock today. "I think you should have a nice cup of 'Opportuni-Tea' today."

"How can I not take your recommendation? You predicted the weather correctly."

"Well, to be honest, it was the smell. I could smell rain, and then I checked my app, and it said there was a sixty percent chance of rain."

"Sure, I'll try the Opportuni-Tea. You've got honey, right?"

"Hon, I have three shelves filled with different types of honey," she waved a hand toward a display of honey, honey pots, and a variety of honey from wildflower to pinecone.

Nicole reviewed the shelf, trying to decide. Zaina turned on the electric kettle and pulled down Nicole's shop mug. Outside of her home, Zaina's shop was Nicole's favorite place to be. There was something so cozy about the small store with its soft lighting, scented candles burning, and the nooks of comfortable chairs that invited you to sit down and read a book or have Zaina read your cards. Light jazz was playing in the background, and Nicole's mind wandered back to Sean. She wondered if he liked music, and if so, what kind?

Zaina edged up to her, "Did you decide on a honey yet?"

"Nah. I'll just take whatever you have open."

Zaina pressed her palms together and tapped her fingers. "Alright, Marley Creek Acacia it is. Now sit down, relax, and tell me all about.. what was his name?"

"Sean," Nicole said quickly.

"Look at that sparkle in your eyes!"

Nicole's face flushed. "This is just silly. He asked me out, and I turned him down. There's nothing to talk about."

Zaina crossed her arms and leveled a commanding stare at her friend. "We've got hours of inventory unpacking, pricing, and tagging. I need this. Tell me everything in glorious detail!"

"Oh, alright, fine. I'll tell you all about it, but it's not that big a deal." Nicole ran a hand through her hair.

By four o'clock, the shelves were stocked, and the inventory tracking system was ready for Zaina's open house next week.

Zaina looked over at her friend slyly. "This year I've added oil-making classes to the open house. We're going to make protection oil, healing oil, even sex oil. You need to come make some sex oil."

Nicole crossed her arms and glared at her friend. "I don't need any sex oil."

"It's not just about the sex, though that would be wonderful for you too. How long has it been?" Zaina cocked her head to the side.

"I don't want to talk about it." Nicole refused to meet Zaina's eyes.

"Okay, a few years then." Zaina pushed a little. "It's healthy to want sex, you know?"

"It's complicated, Zaina. My body...has been through things. You know that."

Zaina put her arm around Nicole. "You of all people should know I believe scars only make us more beautiful. They're proof of our resilience."

Nicole grabbed a tissue and dabbed her eyes. "I don't even know why I am crying."

"My shop brings out emotions. It happens all the time, truly." She gave Nicole a little squeeze.

"Still, I don't need any sex oil. I don't even know if I am going to meet him for tea." Nicole bit her lip.

Zaina beamed, "So, you are going to reach out to him?"

"I think so. I'm not sure? Maybe?" Nicole pressed a finger to her lips in thought.

Zaina hopped up and down. "Come on, please? For me? What do you have to lose?" She stopped begging and said, "If you want, just tell me when you are planning to meet with him and I can go to the coffee shop early and stake the place out. Then if it's bad news, you can give me a nod and I can rescue you."

Nicole twisted her hair in thought. "I don't know, this is all kind of overwhelming and I already told him no, so—"

Zaina gave Nicole puppy-dog eyes.

Nicole rolled her eyes and relented, "Okay fine, but let me sleep on it. I don't even know how to get a hold of him."

"Just call the restaurant!" Zaina said quickly.

Nicole thought about it. "Okay, I'll call the restaurant tomorrow after work."

"And then you'll text me and Devin right away? This is what group chats are made for!"

Nicole laughed. "Of course. You two will be the first, and let me add, only people who will find out how it goes."

"I love it! I've got a good feeling about this, but I'll hold off on the sex oil for now."

Nicole nodded, "Yes, hold off on that for like, ever."

"No way, ma'am. You'll be getting some right after the open house, I think."

"Hey, do you want me to read your cards? See where things are going?" Zaina reached under the counter for her favorite tarot deck and began removing the cards from their bag.

Nicole shook her head from side to side. "No way. First, you know I don't believe. Second, the cards are vague, and I always assume the worst interpretation of the card."

"I wish you wouldn't do that," Zaina said a little sharply, but she put the cards away. "Ready to go? I can give you a ride home."

Nicole walked to the front of the shop, opened the door, and stepped outside. "Looks like the sun came out for sunset. I can walk home."

Zaina and Nicole exchanged a hug, then Zaina pulled back and looked into Nicole's eyes, "You can do this."

"B-b-but," Nicole began.

"Wait, I take that back. Nic, you *deserve* this." Zaina shook her lightly by the shoulders.

Nicole sighed, "I don't know if I can accept it."

"Promise me you'll try," she held out her pinkie, her pointy nails lacquered in black.

Nicole paused for a moment; pinky promises were a sacred trust between their group of three, never entered into lightly. She twisted her pinky with Zaina's and they both sang "Promises, Promises" by Naked Eyes.

"It's set in stone now," Zaina said, wearing a huge grin.

Nicole just waved and started to walk toward her home. "I'll text you."

Zaina walked back into her shop, the bell on the door jingling in the wind.

Thinking about calling and basically asking Sean out tomorrow made her stomach queasy, so she popped in her headphones and began listening to her audiobook. It was the latest book in the long-running cozy mystery series, "The Shirley Sharlock Murders." If anything could distract her, it was Shirley Sharlock and her talking dog, Doc Watson.

She was almost home when she noticed butcher paper was now covering the windows of the old dance studio. Written on the paper in big block letters, it said: *"Coming Soon, "Pupcakes and Clawssants."* Then in smaller writing, *"A bakery for man's (and woman's) best friend."*

Well, that's different, a bakery just for dogs? She wondered if they also would have people baked goods, and what about cats?

Suddenly, the dog bakery door flew open; a woman wearing a baseball hat and paint-splattered overalls stalked out right in front of Nicole. Oblivious to Nicole, the woman continued yelling into her phone.

"At least she isn't on speakerphone," Nicole mumbled to herself.

"You can't be serious! You're leaving me for some guy!? Oh yes, I know he's not just any guy. He's your f-ing ex! God, I don t know what I ever saw in you. It will never last—" she turned to cross the street and saw Nicole. "What are you looking at?" she sneered.

Nicole's jaw dropped. She was speechless.

The woman's face crumbled. She put her phone against her chest and walked toward Nicole. "I'm so sorry. I'm not usually like this. Please don't hold this against me, or my bakery. I can't believe I let her get me so wound up. I'm ranting in the street in front of the business I've dreamed about opening for years." She pressed end and put her phone in the top pocket of her overalls. "I'm sorry, my name is Kate Sterling, and this is my passion project." She gestured at the storefront.

Nicole shook her hand; it was cold and clammy. "Thanks for apologizing. Everyone has bad days. I won't hold it against you."

Kate wiped a hand across her forehead. "Phew! I've only been in Marley Creek for a few weeks. I don't want to start off on the wrong foot."

"I'm sure you haven't. And even if you had, I like to think we are a forgiving bunch. Welcome to town."

"Thank you so much. I appreciate it." Kate adjusted the brim of her hat.

"No worries, I'll let you get back to sorting things out...or painting?" Nicole gestured toward the storefront.

"Thanks. I'm hoping for more painting and less yelling."

"Take care," Nicole said, and continued on her way home.

Chapter Four

♥

Sean stood at the omelet station. Just like yesterday, a long line of patrons waited their turn. He'd been elated to see all the tables full, as well as a line for the buffet. Today, he kept looking at the door, hoping she might come back in. Sean plated another ham and American cheese omelet and then checked his watch. Brunch was almost over. He knew he should stop getting his hopes up, but he just wasn't built that way. He'd always been a glass half full kind of guy. Heck, when he was a kid, his mom always called him her Sunny Sean. Sean cracked a couple of eggs into the waiting pan as he thought about his mom. He had always been a mama's boy who wanted her approval—at least until the divorces started.

Sean, what's with psychoanalysis? Maybe trying to date Nicole was a mistake. She'd said no, and even now he was distracted thinking about her. His priority should continue to be the success of Jesse's Pub. He was building a life and career for himself. He didn't want to wind up like his parents. Both of them could not handle being single and clung to anyone to avoid being alone. He cleaned his station and checked his watch again as a couple of teens in hoodies and pajama pants came up looking for scrambled eggs.

"Scrambled eggs are on the buffet over there." He pointed with his spatula.

"Yeah, but we want them with onions, mushrooms, and tomatoes," said the tallest teen of the group, who tossed his hair in the direction of the vegetables.

"Gotcha, a couple of veggie scrambles coming up." The teens went back to their phones, and Sean got to work. He should have given Nicole his phone number, or better yet, he should've asked to enter it into her phone. Jasper would have done that.

The teens had been the last patrons in line. Sean looked around the dining room once more, just in case Nicole had slipped in while he'd been scrambling some eggs. His heart leapt. A woman with wavy auburn hair and a jean jacket was picking up an order. Could it be her? He quickly took off his gloves and rushed to the counter.

"It's okay, I got it," he said to the server who was about to process the order. He stepped around the counter and said, "Thanks for giving us a second chance—" He stopped when he saw who he was looking at. A woman wearing a Southern Illinois University Mom T-shirt stared at him quizzically.

"Oh, I'm so sorry, Ma'am. I thought you were someone else."

"No problem," she said and handed him her platinum card.

Sean shook his head and mumbled to himself, "You need to get a grip and focus on the job at hand." He gave himself a shake and then went from table to table in the dining room and on the patio to make sure everyone was enjoying their brunch and to thank them for coming into Jesse's. He tried to take his own advice and focus on the attitude of gratitude he'd heard discussed on the *How to Make Your Restaurant Wildly Successful* podcast. By the time the last brunch patron had left, he was energized, focused, and not thinking about the cute spray of freckles on the bridge of Nicole's nose. *Oh, who was I kidding?*

He needed a fun, non-threatening way to approach her again, and he needed her to give him a chance. One date, one tea, was all he was asking for. He walked into the kitchen to make himself a cup of tea and review his menu for this week's halftime buffet. Three kinds of flatbreads, mini sliders, and the yard-long charcuterie board should work for the football crowd.

"That's it!" he shouted.

"What's it?" Mable said from right behind him.

"Oh, nothing. Just an idea I had."

"Is it about the woman from the brunch yesterday? The one who turned you down?"

"How do you know about that?" His lips turned down and his ears got hot.

"I know all," she said with dramatic flair.

"So, it would seem," he said deadpan as he knocked food debris off serving spoons into the trash.

"What's your plan?" Mable asked enthusiastically.

Sean brightened. Maybe she could give him some advice on whether his gift idea would work. "Here is what I was thinking. I'd make a little charcuterie board with a Denver omelet theme. Think deconstructed Denver omelet. Some Canadian bacon, pearl onions, Peppadew peppers, smoked gouda, and a couple of deviled eggs. What do you think?"

"That sounds amazing! Make me one too!"

"Sure, be here by eleven tomorrow."

"I've got school." She tossed her rag into the laundry bin.

"Bummer for you."

"Hey! You knew that when you offered!"

Sean laughed.

"Now I'm not going to help you write a card for your gift."

"Who said I needed your help?"

Mable flipped her ponytail and crossed her arms. "You don't have to say it. It's obvious. When's the last time you asked someone out?"

"It's been quite a while."

"I know. Now, let me help." She put her palms together, begging.

"Thank you," he said, his shoulders relaxing. Less than twenty minutes later, his note was written.

"When are you going to drop this off at the school?"

"I don't know what time her lunch is, so I thought noon should work."

"Nah, that's too late. What if you drop it off and she's already gone to lunch? Then she won't be hungry. You should go there at eleven. That way all the kids will be in class, plus there won't be teachers hanging out in the office, and she'll be getting hungry."

"Mable, you're a genius!"

"You need to remember that, Sean! But seriously, I'm the oldest of six kids. I think I've spent more time at Ida B. Wells Elementary than some parents."

"Did I say you're the best already?"

"No, and even if you did, you can say it again."

"Thank you, Mable. You're the best."

"I know. Now you better tell me what happens. I want to know the second I walk in on Wednesday. And wear a Henley."

"What!?"

"Women love a man in a Henley and a decent pair of jeans that hug—"

"Stop right there! I get it!"

Mable laughed and carried a tray of rolled silverware out to the dining room.

Chapter Five

♥

Nicole stared at her face in the mirror. She'd applied concealer to the dark circles under her eyes, but it wasn't concealing anything. She'd tossed and turned all night, trying to decide what she was going to say to Sean. Maybe it wasn't such a good idea to start dating again. Wait, is that what she was doing? Her eyes were wide; the whites of her brown eyes overtaking her irises. She'd only gone out once since Duncan had broken their engagement, and that had been a complete and total drunken disaster.

But she had pinky promised, and she didn't think Zaina would understand if she didn't go through with making that phone call. Was she ready to lose a friendship over one phone call? Maybe Sean would tell her, "No, thank you." She took out her eyeshadow and began doing her eyes. She hadn't even considered that Sean probably hadn't thought twice about her saying no to him. For all he knew, she might have a boyfriend, or girlfriend, for that matter. The prospect of him no longer being interested in her should have flooded her with relief, and it mostly did, but deep down a spark of 'what if' resided.

She brushed mascara onto her lashes and thought about those dimples. He had a lovely smile. She'd like to see that smile again and maybe kiss his full lips; however unlikely that might be. If she could find a way to reach deep down and hold on to that spark, she could make the phone call. She checked her phone for the time. It wasn't even seven-thirty yet. Too bad she couldn't call right now and get it over with since she had talked herself into it.

She put on her ID lanyard and walked out the front door, checking to make sure it locked behind her. As she walked around the corner to Ida B. Wells Elementary, she listened to her favorite autumn playlist. The opening notes of "this is what autumn feels like" by JVKE immediately slowed her racing thoughts. The orchestral production and the plaintive singing voice always moved her. She tapped the repeat button on her phone. This was the only song she wanted in her ears this morning. A public works truck was loaded with pumpkins and cornstalks; they were decorating the space around the town sign. One of the many things she loved about her hometown was that they really did it up for the holidays. The only celebration that outshone the fall festivities was the annual Mistletoe Market, which was held the first weekend in December.

Nicole smiled. She loved Christmas. As far as she was concerned, the Christmas season could start October first. *Zaina would hate that*, Nicole thought, just as her phone pinged. *Speak of the devil*, Nicole read the text from Zaina, which was quickly followed by a text from Devin.

Z: You got this!

DEV: Z is right. You can do this beautiful friend.

Nicole sent back a heart hands emoji and walked into work.

***

Sean placed the notecard in its envelope and affixed it to the top of the takeout box with a piece of tape. He ripped up the nine other attempts at the notecard and paused over the recycling bin before deciding that the only place he wanted them was in the trash. Nervously, he started tucking in his Henley before he remembered Mable's strict instructions for it to remain untucked. The clock on the stove showed it was already quarter to eleven. "Time to go," he said to his betta fish, Hermie.

Sean got in his ancient Jeep Wrangler and drove to the school. He snagged the only open visitor space and then checked his phone. He'd made it to the school with seven minutes to spare. Butterflies fluttered in his stomach as he realized he hadn't considered what he was going to say when he dropped off Nicole's lunch. Should he stay while she read the card? Maybe he should have had it delivered. He didn't want to make Nicole feel uncomfortable or like she had to say yes to him.

He turned off the Jeep and reminded himself what he was good at: hoping for the best, winging it, and cooking fantastic food. "Sean, you got this! It's gonna work out." With pep in his step, he made his way to the entrance door of the school and pressed the doorbell. A moment later, the outer door buzzed, and he walked into the vestibule.

"How can we help you?" a voice said through a speaker.

"I have a delivery for Nicole..." *Crap*, Sean thought. *I should have googled and tried to find out her last name, but man, I don't want to seem like a stalker.* His palms were sweating. "It's from Jesse's Pub."

Buzz.

And he was in.

A smiling woman wearing glasses sat at the front desk. "Nicole never orders out," she said and reached out for the bag.

"Is she not here?"

"Do you need payment or something? I hope she tipped on the app." Her brow furrowed.

"No, no, nothing like that. This is actually a gift."

"Oh, how wonderful! I'll make sure she gets it right away!"

Sean attempted to surreptitiously look around the office for any sign of Nicole.

The woman at the front desk leaned to the side and made eye contact with Sean.

"Is that all?" She said with finality.

Yikes, thought Sean, *she must think I'm a creep or something.*

"Yes, Ma'am." He nodded.

"Have a nice day," she said and pressed the automatic door. It swung open and Sean exited as quickly as possible.

He got back in his Jeep and headed home. He spent the next several hours going over inventory reports and placing orders with his meat and dairy suppliers. Instead of his usual laser focus on his work and making sure all the numbers were balanced, he could not get Nicole out of his head. Did she eat the lunch he made? What did she think of the note? Would she call him? Text him? What if she didn't respond at all? This was not like him. First of all, why was he worried? Of course, she'd call or text him. She was a nice person. She wasn't the type of person who wouldn't bother to say thank you, even if she wasn't interested. Too bad Mable was in class; otherwise, he'd text her to give her the update and maybe she'd be able to talk him off the ledge he'd been perched on.

He heard his phone vibrate and ran over to the counter where it was charging.

> Our records show that you are due for a six month teeth cleaning. Please call Dr. Dave today at 800-GOT-EETH or click **here**!

"Ugh!" he groaned and then clicked to schedule his cleaning. Sean made a note on his calendar, and then it was time to give Hermie his special betta fish food.

"Hey buddy, what do you think? Think she'll go out with me? I agree. I am quite the catch. Oh yes, I see what you did there. Nice pun, buddy. I'm losing my mind here, Hermie. I'm going to go work in the garden."

Sean drove the short distance from his apartment over to the restaurant. Right behind the restaurant was his pride and joy—a small group of three raised garden beds and a compost bin. The season was winding down, but his herbs were still producing well. He was hoping to keep the sage, thyme, and lavender going outdoors until December, but he was going to need to start transplanting some herbs into pots to move indoors for the winter.

He talked to his plants as he watered and weeded, thanking the heirloom tomato plants for being especially productive this year. It looked like he'd be able to harvest some deep purple beets this week, just in time for the special menu he was working on for Jasper's Oktoberfest kick-off dinner. "Y'all look fantastic and are going to be delicious as a side with some vinegar and caraway seeds." His stomach rumbled; he'd forgotten to eat lunch.

If anyone overheard him, they'd probably think he was crazy for talking to his plants; then again, these days they might assume that he had headphones in and was on his phone. Speaking of his phone, he'd left it in his Jeep so he could focus on his garden, and now he was itching to see if Nicole had contacted him. He quickly put away his gardening tools.

His stomach growled again, and he considered going inside to make himself a sandwich, but he tried not to go into the restaurant when it was closed. It was too easy for him to pop in for a quick second and then find himself leaving hours later. He'd experienced restaurant burnout before, and that had led to a bout of mono and the loss of his first executive chef job. He wasn't going down that path again. "Work to live, not live to work," he said and walked past the front door of Jesse's Pub and over to where he had parked.

As soon as he got in the driver's seat, he picked up his phone and there it was, a text from a local number that wasn't assigned to a contact. It was her! His stomach churned as he unlocked his phone; he hadn't been this nervous about a girl since he was in high school.

> Hi Sean! Thank you for a delish lunch! Tomorrow at four works for me!

Sorry, this is Nicole, in case you didn't know who it was.

His chest felt like it was going to burst; he was so excited. She said yes to the date!

SEAN: Great! Can't wait to see you at Common Grounds tomorrow at four. (Smiley face emoji)

He tossed the phone back into the passenger's seat and drove home singing along with the radio. Sean had a good feeling about this, about her.

Chapter Six

Nicole walked back into the office and plopped down in front of her desk. A takeout box sat on top of her keyboard. A card with her name on it was attached to the top of the box.

"What's this?" she asked her co-worker, Nancy.

"Delivery from Jesse's Pub. He said it was a gift." Nancy rushed to answer as the office phone rang.

Nicole's heart thumped. Could it be from Sean? It had to be! No one else would send her something from Jesse's pub. If this was some sort of motivational ploy from Devin to get her to call Sean, she was going to kill her.

She opened the envelope and pulled out the card. Opening it, she didn't even read the words; she just scanned down to the signature at the bottom, Sean H. Her breath quickened with excitement. "Oh my gosh," Nicole whispered. "Oh my gosh, oh my gosh."

After a deep breath, she read the note from Sean:

Dear Nicole:

I'm afraid I might have come across a little too strong the other day. I prepared this charcuterie to apologize, and I'm looking for another opportunity to ask you out for tea.

Are you free tomorrow afternoon? Say 4pm? If that doesn't work for you, we can pick another time.

If I don't hear from you in the next couple of days, I'll assume I got my wires crossed and you aren't interested.

Hope to hear from you soon.

Yours,

Sean H.

312-555-1212

She traced the word yours with her finger and then opened the box and took a picture of the lunch to send to the group chat.

NIC: You will not believe what just happened!

DEV: Do tell…

Z: Did you talk to Sean?

She sent the picture to the group and replied.

NIC: No, but he sent me this and a note.

DEV: Charcuterie, nice. What are the roses?

NIC: Not sure I'll take a bite.

NIC: prosciutto

DEV: Let me get this straight—he sent you a charcuterie plate with prosciutto, onions, peppers, and deviled eggs?

NIC: Yes! And some gouda cheese.

DEV: Hon, he sent you a deconstructed Denver omelet! You need to marry that man.

NIC: STOP

DEV: I'm just saying, he's handsome, he likes you, and he can cook!

Z: Devin, don't freak her out with marriage talk!

DEV: Alright, alright, but you *are* going to go on a date with him, right, Nic?

NIC: I promised Z I'd call him. At least now I know he still wants to meet for tea.

Z: True!

DEV: So when is the first date?

NIC: Don't stress me out, Devin! Tomorrow, just for tea.

DEV: I'll take it!

Z: I have a good feeling about this.

NIC: Z, you better not be pulling out your tarot cards!

Z: Who, me? Never.

NIC: Z!

Z: What? Okay, I'll respect your opinion. I won't pull any cards for you and Sean—for now.

NIC: Thank you.

Z: But maybe you can find out his birthday, and if possible, when he was born. Like if you can just find out what time of day? I can work with that.

NIC: ZAINA NO!

DEV: LOL, I gotta get back to work. I've got the condo board meeting for that building next to Hop's Heaven. There was a fistfight in their parking lot Sat. night.

NIC: Ugh!

Z: Boo!

DEV: Nic, I'll call you after the twins are asleep to go over your outfit for the big date.

NIC: Thanks, Dev.

Nicole set the phone down and began eating the meal Sean had made for her. She had to admit that no guy had ever done anything like this for her before. The prosciutto roses were preferable to the kind that sat in a vase and died. She'd like to get used to this. There were a few minutes left before she had to resume working, so she unlocked her phone to respond to Sean. She carefully typed in Sean's number and then she triple-checked it before typing in her reply:

Thanks for the delicious lunch. Tomorrow at four sounds great.

She read it over, deleted it, and retyped it.

Hi Sean! Thank you for a delish lunch! Tomorrow at 4 works for me!

Nicole worried her bottom lip and started to delete the new message, and then she stopped.

"Don't overthink," she said to herself, and hit send. Then she over thought and added a second text:

Sorry, this is Nicole, in case you didn't know who it was.

Nancy cleared her throat and rolled her chair over so she was next to Nicole. "I haven't seen you smile that wide in I don't know how long! Spill the beans, Nicole!"

Nicole opened her mouth to respond, but Nancy continued talking.

"Who sent you lunch?" Nancy said, sliding her reading glasses down so she could see Nicole's face better. "You know, I live vicariously through you single people. I've been married for 35 years now. I need to hear about young love." Nancy propped her hand on her chin and waited for Nicole to speak. "We've got some time before the afternoon kindergarten rush. Now is the perfect time to chat."

Nicole rolled her eyes. "There isn't much to tell."

"So you say, but your eyes are all twinkly and you're still smiling. What's his name?"

"Okay, fine. It's Sean."

"Go on."

"He is the owner of Jesse's Pub."

"That's nice. Bud and I have gotten takeout from there a few times. Yummy stuff. I don't know that I've seen the owner. What does he look like?"

Nicole tilted her head. "Let's see, he's at least six feet tall. He has that hairstyle where it's kind of longish on top and shorter on the sides. His hair is dark brown, and his face has stubble from not shaving for a few days. Also, he has dimples and an amazing smile."

"Oh!" It dawned on Nancy and she snapped her fingers. "Your Sean is the one who brought the food! Aww, he brought you lunch. How long have you two been dating?"

"We aren't," she blurted.

"Okay, what's the scoop then?"

"We're going to meet for tea tomorrow after work. He asked if I wanted to go for coffee originally, but I can't do caffeine late in the day, so I'll be ordering an herbal tea. I wonder what he will order? Do you know if Common Grounds still has a daily scone? I haven't had a scone in forever. I usually don't get them. They are filled with gobs of butter, but they're always dry. I think I'd rather have a cookie or a donut, like a nice cake donut, or even a Danish."

Nancy clapped her hands, "Nicole, you're babbling."

Nicole's cheeks flushed, "Sorry about that."

"Hon, don't apologize. I hope the date goes well. He seems like a decent guy, and you deserve a good guy, especially after..." she paused.

"Ugh, don't even utter his name!"

Nancy pantomimed zipping her lips and throwing away the key, and then the bell rang.

Nicole checked her phone, but no reply from Sean. "Back to work," she said.

The reason Nicole had clung to working as much as possible when she was going through chemo was because of her longing for normalcy, but it was also because working at the school was non-stop. Work was the only place she could turn off her brain. Surrounded by a sea of kids learning and playing, plus all the interacting with the parents, she had no time to think of herself.

She was in awe of the love the parents had for their kids. School was wildly hectic and yet, for her, a rare peaceful place. As the last bus pulled out of the parking lot, she opened her desk drawer and pulled out her purse. She fished out her keys and said goodbye to Nancy. There was no way she was going to check her phone in front of her. She walked out into the afternoon sunshine and began walking home. As soon as she was out of the school parking lot, she pulled out her phone. There was a new text from Sean. She halted, her hands shaking as she unlocked her phone to read what he had to say.

> Sean Harper: Great! Can't wait to see you at Common Grounds tomorrow at 4. (smiley face emoji).

Nicole was so filled with energy she couldn't help herself from having a little skip in her step as she crossed the empty lot on her corner. She spent the rest of her walk thinking of what to say next. She walked up her front steps and plopped into the patio chair on her front porch.

> Nicole: It's a date! (heart eyes emoji.)

Her thumb hovered over the send button. Should she send heart eyes? Was it a bit much? She backspaced and added the basic smiley emoji. Hopefully, their tea would go so well the next time she sent a text she would be able to add heart eyes, or even the blow a kiss emoji.

Chapter Seven

♥

He'd spent the day at Jesse's putting together the schedule for the next week. The Oktoberfest events he was collaborating on with Hop's Heaven meant he needed to have staff at the restaurant and staff for the food stand over at Jasper's place. It was going to be tight, especially with his sous chef, Charlie, being unreliable as of late. He needed to look for someone to replace Charlie. Sean had printed out a help wanted sign and taped it in the window of Jesse's, and printed one to hang up on the community board over at Common Grounds.

Sean had showered and shaved for his date. Wisely, he followed Mable's fashion tips from the other day. He'd put on a light grey Henley, paired with his favorite faded jeans. With wallet, keys, and phone in hand, he gave himself the once-over in the mirror before feeding Hermie and heading out the door He was running early as usual, so he put on his David Bowie playlist and took the long way into town from his apartment.

The leaves were beginning to change, and there wasn't a cloud in the sky, making it a perfect day to drive around Marley Lake and then into town. As he drove around, he saw a few people out fishing at the community pier. The lake was strictly catch and release; you had to be on the lookout for turtles as, for whatever reason; the lake was teeming with them.

When he drove along the east side of the lake, he noticed a few kids were playing on the Lake Park playground, as well as couples walking along the bike path. If the weather stayed nice, he could take Nicole on a date here. They could go for a walk around the lake and then have a little picnic. He had a nice bottle of wine he'd been saving for a special occasion. What could be better than sharing it with her?

He turned up the volume and sang along with David Bowie. The sun was shining. It was warm, but not hot, and he was on his way to spend time with a beautiful woman. Life was good. A few minutes later, he pulled up in front of Common Grounds and parked his Jeep. It was a quarter to four, so he had time to hang up his help wanted sign and pick a suitable spot to sit with Nicole.

He found a small, high-top table for two facing the door that was away from the counter and tucked next to a door to a small private room. This would give them some privacy to talk freely with no one overhearing them. He checked his phone quickly just in case Nicole had tried to text him. She hadn't. Now he just needed to wait. Sean had a feeling the next few minutes were going to take an eternity.

Ding. The door chimed, and Sean's head popped up expectantly. It was only a noisy group of pre-teen girls, so he turned his attention to his phone and started scrolling on his social media. Now would be a good time to make a couple of posts for Jesse's Pub, but his concentration at the moment was wavering. Butterflies had filled his stomach and now they were making their way into his arms and legs. He bounced his leg under the table. *Ding.* A delivery driver came in and picked up an order. *Third time's a charm,* he thought nervously.

Ding. The door opened, and there she was. Her cheeks were flushed, and she looked around nervously.

He smiled and waved. "Nicole!"

She walked over to the table. He loved her eyes and the way they crinkled when she smiled. Her hair bounced as she walked, and he imagined how soft it would feel when—yes, when, and not if—he ran his hand through her hair and pulled her to him, kissing her slowly and gently. He wanted to taste her.

He got up and moved around the table. "Is it alright to give you a hug? I'm a hugger."

Nicole nodded and entered his warm embrace. She smelled of vanilla and jasmine with just a hint of spice. She gave him a small squeeze and stepped back. He quickly pulled out her chair, and she smiled and sat down.

He moved back around to his chair and sat down. "Hi," he said brightly.

"Hi." Her eyes gleamed in a way he'd not seen before. She twisted a lock of her auburn hair.

They both looked at each other for a moment, smiling nervous smiles, unsure of who should speak first. "What?" they both said, and then they laughed.

"Ladies first." Sean nodded toward her.

"What are you thinking about getting?" Nicole asked him, leaning forward.

"I'm going to try their brown sugar iced tea latte."

"Oh, that sounds good," she said.

"How about you?" He leaned his head toward her.

"I'm going to stick with my tried and true and get their herbal mint tea with a splash of almond milk and honey."

"Solid plan. You stay here, and I'll go place our order." He tapped the table with his wallet and stood up.

"Sounds great." She sat up straighter in her seat, and as he walked up to the counter, she turned in her seat. She noticed how great he looked in those jeans.

Sean walked to the counter and placed their order. As he was waiting, he looked at the bakery case. Banana bread was his favorite, so he got a slice of that as well as a pumpkin muffin because, well, it was fall, and he knew Common Grounds used local pumpkins.

Sean balanced the baked goods and their drinks in his arms and made his way back to the table. He let out a sigh of relief when he saw Nicole wasn't on her phone. He hadn't been on a ton of dates in the last couple of years, but he'd been on enough to know that when someone was on their phone during a date, it wasn't going well. With a little pep in his step, he returned to their table. He had a good feeling about this date.

***

Nicole stood up to help Sean put down the food and drinks.

"I thought I'd get us a snack to go with our drinks. I hope you like banana bread or pumpkin muffins."

Nicole nodded vigorously. "Love them, and to be honest, I don't think I've ever met a baked good I didn't like."

Sean chuckled, "My kind of girl."

Nicole warmed at the thought of being his girl. Maybe Zaina was right; maybe it was time for her to live, or at least let someone new into her small life. She smiled as Sean sliced each of the treats in equal halves, then plated them and served her first, then himself.

"I feel so pampered," she said and then realized no date, no boyfriend, not even her ex-fiancé had plated food for her. Sure, it was a recycled paper plate and a compostable spork; nevertheless, she felt cared for in a way she hadn't felt since she was a kid at her Grandma's house. For a change, she allowed herself to feel the good feeling, being comfortable in this man's presence.

His dimples popped as he smiled and raised his mug to hers, "To second chances."

"To amazing charcuterie," she said with mock seriousness.

"I'm so happy you enjoyed it," he said, his chest puffed a little. She looked at his open collar, noticing a dusting of dark hair and the way the shirt accented his biceps. Either he did a lot of lifting at Jesse's Pub—which she didn't doubt—or he found time to go to the gym. She'd like to slide her hand up under his shirt and feel the muscles of his chest, and then move her hands slowly down, lightly brush one of his nipples—.

"Well, what do you think?" He asked, drawing her out of her head and back into their conversation.

She panicked for a moment, unsure what he was talking about. He took a spork full of banana bread and placed it in his mouth.

"I think it's pretty good, but I'd like it better if it had walnuts." She held her breath, hoping she'd answered the right question.

He chewed, "I think you're right." He hesitated, then added, "Now that we're here, I realize that for the last few years I've only gone on dates with people I've been messaging for a while before the date. I think I've forgotten how to do this whole," he waved his spork, "first date thing. You're a totally blank canvas. I know nothing about you!"

Nicole smiled a little sadly. She thought to herself, *What should I share? What will scare him away? Should I even be here?* In her mind she could hear Devin say she doesn't owe him anything, and she is worthy of happiness.

"Here's the thing," she said, "it's been a long time since I've gone on any dates."

"No worries. We can figure this out together."

Relief flooded Nicole; maybe she didn't have to tell Sean all about Duncan leaving and the cancer. Not today, at least. It would be nice for one date to feel normal and not have to explain how she was broken.

"Wonderful," said Nicole. "So we know where each of us works. I guess we can talk about family, or where are you from? You pick."

Sean rubbed his scruff. "I moved to Marley Creek three years ago. I'm originally from Michigan, a few hours away from here in a town called Kalamazoo."

"How did you wind up here in Marley Creek?"

"I met Jasper Kane from Hop's Heaven at a conference for concept taverns and pubs, and we hit it off. He invited me to come out to Marley Creek and intern with him for the summer while he was opening Hop's Heaven." He leaned in, "Not to brag, but it was my idea to repurpose a railroad car for the outdoor space to house a second bar that was easy to open and close without being dependent on the weather."

"Well done, you!" Nicole leaned in and patted his shoulder. As she did, she noticed Sean's eyes dip down to get a closer look at her cleavage. Normally, any guy looking at her chest made her self-conscious, but in Sean's case, it sent a thrill down her spine.

"After I'd been in Marley Creek for a few weeks, I knew I'd found my home. We've got the lake and the train, plus a downtown that is just one gazebo short of a Hallmark movie town."

Nicole gasped. "You watch the Hallmark Channel?"

Sean raised his glass. "Is it even the holiday season without Hallmark?"

Nicole tapped her mug to his. "Exactly. I love that you watch Hallmark movies," she said enthusiastically.

Sean nodded, "It's become a holiday tradition." His smile disappeared, and he became quiet. "When my parents got divorced, my mom got Christmas and my dad got Thanksgiving. His first new wife couldn't stand football, so throughout Thanksgiving weekend we'd watch Hallmark Christmas movies instead of the NFL. We'd eat the leftovers and watch the big city girl come home to the small town and fall in love with a farmer. Looking back, I understand now that I would have enjoyed whatever we were watching because it was time spent with my dad. But those simple stories of people finding a happily ever-after while surrounded by all the best things about Christmas, that became a tradition that I clung to, especially when I was a teenager because by then my family life wasn't stable."

Sean's openness as he shared his love of silly Christmas movies and the quiet way he talked about his family's imperfections made Nicole's heart feel like it was expanding in her chest. Should she dare to imagine snuggling with Sean, watching a Hallmark movie while it snowed outside? What would it be like to have him in her kitchen packing lunch for her on a school day? What would it be like to bask in his light every day?

"How about you? What's your Hallmark movie origin story?" He leaned back to listen to her fully.

Anxiety flooded her body. Hallmark movies had gotten her through chemotherapy. She'd watched Hallmark exclusively during every one of her infusion treatments. Thankfully, unlike certain foods, chemo hadn't ruined her love of happy endings. She'd hoped to avoid any talk of it today, but unfortunately, cancer was part of her story for the rest of her life. She steeled herself to answer.

"I wish mine was as sweet as yours. Your story could be made into a Hallmark movie. In fact, I wouldn't be surprised if it already was!"

Sean cocked his head, "I hadn't thought of that, but I think you're right!"

"A couple of years ago I was very sick and had to have months of treatment. Hallmark Christmas movies helped me get through all of those crappy days. Once I got better and the Countdown to Christmas started again, I was afraid that watching the movies might give me PTSD. Thank goodness I was wrong about that and they remain the best cozy escape for me."

Sean reached over and put his hand on top of hers, "I'm glad being sick didn't wreck Hallmark movies for you. I mean, I'd totally understand if it did. But most importantly, are you all good now?"

She reached over with her other hand and squeezed his, "Yep, I'm all good, I mean as much as any of us can be," she said with a small, winsome smile, not quite meeting his eyes. She hoped that not being too specific about having had breast cancer and the aftermath of it was okay on a first date. "Well now, that all the fun has been sucked out of the date by me, please let me change the topic." She went to remove her hand from his, and he gently grabbed it.

"Please don't apologize for telling me about yourself. I'm an eternal optimist—but I don't need stuff sugar-coated. I want to get to know you. All of you." His eyes bored into hers.

She shivered under his intense gaze. She didn't know how to react to his interest in her. His kindness. What had she done to deserve this? It was too much. She felt overwhelmed.

"You're making me blush," she said, trying to play off the seriousness of his words. She pulled back her hand and changed the topic.

"Your name is Sean, so why is your restaurant called Jesse's Pub?"

He laughed. "That's a great question. I'm actually amazed that more people don't ask me about the name."

"Points for me." Nicole quipped.

"You have so many points, all of them good."

She fanned herself. "Thank you, thank you. Now, what's the scoop on the name?"

"Jesse was my best friend when I was a kid," he shrugged. "My golden retriever. She was a divorce gift. I was ten when my dad moved out, and the first time he visited after that, he brought me Jesse. My mom was not happy, and that was putting it mildly. But Jesse and I bonded from that first night, and for the next ten years we were inseparable. Thank goodness for that because my parents went from one relationship to another, and Jesse was my rock. Thinking about it, I'd even say Jesse was a big factor in why I went to a community college. I wasn't ready to leave my dog."

Nicole was a pile of mush. "Aww, that's the sweetest story ever. I love that you named your place after your childhood pet. So cute! You should tell that story to everyone you date."

He barked a laugh, "Right now, I'm only interested in impressing one woman."

Her face heated again. She looked over at the window and realized the sun was setting. They'd been sitting there for hours. She should go.

She turned back to Sean.

His knee bounced under the table again. "B-but seriously, these days, I don't have the time to have a dog, so it's just me and my betta fish, Hermie."

Nicole giggled, "Hermie is a great fish name."

Sean grinned. "Did you have a pet growing up?"

"We had a cat at my house, no dogs. His name was Jenks, but he was more my mom's pet than mine. Jenks was around before I was born, so he was pretty old by the time I was in grade school. He was a mean old cat; he used to bite anyone besides my mom who tried to pet him. I learned quickly not to cuddle him. These days," she shrugged, "I don't know. I suppose I have time for a dog, but I wouldn't even know where to begin. Not that I don't like them! "

Sean put a hand over his heart, "Phew, that would be a deal breaker for sure."

"Glad I passed the test," Nicole said.

Sean looked at her with that unwavering intensity again. "You most certainly have."

Butterflies filled her stomach. Maybe she could do this. She spoke, "I was wondering —"

"No, Daddy!" Sean and Nicole turned to see a family standing at the counter. A mom was holding a chubby baby with dark curly hair in the cutest little overalls, and a dad was down at eye level attempting to reason with a toddler over a cake pop.

Sean chuckled. "I think he's got his work cut out for him. She's as cute as a button." Nicole looked at the family and back at Sean. She thought he had a wistful look on his face. He was probably looking forward to having kids of his own one day. Why wouldn't he, right?

That was something she didn't have left to give. Her eyes began to sting a little. She covered it up with a small cough, and Sean returned his eyes to her.

"I'm sorry about that. What were you about to say?"

Nicole cleared her throat. She didn't belong with him. It would be better for them both for her to nip this in the bud.

"I was wondering if you were ready to go?"

"Oh," Sean said, his face scrunched up in confusion. He turned over his phone. "Wow, it's eight o'clock. We've been here quite a while."

"And it's a school night," Nicole said. She pushed out her chair and stood up. She started to put on her jacket.

Sean came around. "Here, let me help you." He came close behind her and held up her coat.

As Nicole put her arm into the sleeve, she couldn't help but inhale a whiff of his scent. It was woodsy with a hint of citrus, like he'd washed his hair with lemon-scented shampoo after an afternoon of chopping wood. Her resolve faltered. Maybe she was getting ahead of herself. Maybe they could date or just be friends. Then she heard the baby gurgling. *Nope*, she thought.

"Thanks," she said, and Sean put his hand on her back.

"Here, let me walk you to the door. Did you park out front?"

"I walked. Gotta get those steps in, you know?" she said collegially.

"I guess," he said flatly, "let me give you a ride home."

She paused as they stepped out of the café. "That's not necessary. I walk all the time."

"It's dark. I'm sure it's fine, but please," he insisted, "Let me drop you off at home so I know you made it home safe."

"Ok."

The ride to Nicole's house was quiet. The awkwardness was so thick in the jeep she could hardly breathe. Fortunately, her house was only a few minutes from the coffee shop. While they waited for the stoplight on Main Street, Nicole struggled for something to say. "Are you looking forward to Halloween?" she asked. She could have smacked her forehead; what a dumb question.

"I'm not much for Halloween. This year, Jasper asked me to do a pairing dinner, so I'll be at Hop's Heaven for his Gourmet

Ghost Gathering. I'll also be at Jasper's for trivia night this week, so we are going to test out a few appetizers for the fall menu."

"Gourmet Ghost Gathering, that's quite a mouthful," she said.

Sean rolled his eyes. "Tell me about it."

He pulled into her driveway, and she had her seatbelt off the moment the Jeep was in park. She opened the door and hopped out before Sean could get his seatbelt off and walk around to open her door.

"Well, ah, I guess I'll see you around then?" he asked.

Looking at his fallen face, she felt so bad. *No,* she told herself; it was better this way for both of them. He'd realize that soon enough. "Thank you again. I had a nice time! Yes, I suppose I'll see you around town." Then she turned and speed-walked up to her house. It was so cold and uninviting after the hours spent in Sean's warmth.

Nicole heard him engage the clutch as opened her door. She wanted to turn around and yell, "Wait! I think I might be making a mistake! Maybe we can do this?" But it was too late, and he was already down the road. This was for the best, wasn't it? She closed the door behind her and locked it. Nicole should be happy. After not going on a date in years, she'd gone, and it had been nice. Marriage, a family—these things weren't in the cards for her anymore, and that's just how it was. She was just lucky to be alive and not have cancer anymore. Every day she got now was a bonus.

Chapter Eight

♥

The next morning, she swiped open her phone and noticed a couple of messages had come from her newly renamed group chat. The group chat was now *We need the* deets, *Nicole.* Nicole chuckled. She needed the laugh this morning.

> DEV: As a courtesy to you, and because I fell asleep while reading a bedtime story to the twins, I've waited until the morning to text you.

> Z: I hope you woke up with a hot chef in bed next to you. You deserve fantastic sex on the first date.

Nicole considered leaving the text on read. She hadn't been able to sleep until after three, which caused her to oversleep. Now she had ten minutes to get out the door for work. She wished she were running late because she'd had sex with Sean the night before. The truth was so sad in comparison. Her throat tightened and her eyes filled with tears. She was just so tired. Why did everything have to be so hard?

She shouldn't have tried. It was safer to be alone. She had friends, a job she loved, and she was currently in great health. A life partner just wasn't in the cards for her. One thing she'd learned during cancer treatment was no matter how shitty she felt physically or mentally, or how painful life might be, she only had two choices, and one was to die. This was small potatoes compared to when Duncan left. This was nothing compared to having to tell her mom she had breast cancer. This was a minor blip. She tried a date, and it didn't work out. Onward.

Bolstered by her thoughts, she replied to the group chat.

> NIC: It was ok I don't think there will be a second date. (shrug emoji)

> Z: Oh nooo! This won't do, Nic! Mike is working late so I'm free. Dev, do you have time tonight?

> DEV: Councilman Sanchez is having a town hall meeting, I said I'd attend, but I should be done by eight?

> Z: Nic, mind if we come over? I'll bring that hard cider you like...

Nicole thought about her answer as she finished walking to work. She didn't know if she wanted to rehash the date with Sean; but at the same time, she valued what her friends had to say. Without them, she'd literally be dead. She sat down on the steps of one of the playground slides and texted back.

> NIC: Sure, any excuse to see my bestie! XOXO

With that decided, she put her phone in her purse and headed into work where she would hopefully spend the day not thinking about Sean. Who was she kidding? She took a deep breath, buzzed herself into the school where the halls were filled with small kids and loud voices.

***

Wednesday was half-price buttermilk-brined fried chicken night at Jesse's Pub. The special was for dine-in only, and that meant Jesse's was packed from the moment they opened at four p.m. until they closed at ten p.m. when the last couple paid their bill. Those senior citizens sure love a special. Sean loved Wednesday because he never had waitstaff calling off on that day. There wasn't a restaurant nearby that could compete with the load of tips they all brought home Wednesday nights. Plus, Sean always made a few extra batches of his chicken for the staff to take home after work. It was delicious cold the next day, and they could use it for chicken salad.

This Wednesday, however, Sean found himself in a bit of a mood. That mood had a name, and it was '*what the heck Nicole*'. Sean began pulling out the tubs of chicken that had been brining overnight in the cooler. He set them on the counter by the sink and pulled out an industrial-sized strainer. Carefully, he began dumping the tubs into the strainer while his mind tried to figure things out.

It had all been going so well! He hadn't laughed so much in years. She seemed so open and interested. He knew he wasn't imagining their connection. True, she wasn't as into him as he was into her, but he knew she felt the spark, and then—Poof! She was cold. He'd tossed and turned all night trying to figure out if it was something he'd said, but he'd come up with nothing.

He pulled out his tongs and trays. He added eggs to the first tray and whisked them. Then he added flour to the second along with his special seasoning blend of parsley, sage, rosemary, and thyme. In the last tray, he added pulverized salt and vinegar chips—his secret ingredient. Working quickly, he began breading twelve dozen pieces of chicken to start. The two sides that accompanied the half-off chicken special, coleslaw and potato salad, had been prepped the day before and were sitting in the cooler ready for portioning out.

His phone chimed. He looked at his watch and saw a text from Jasper.

> JASPER: You're still coming out tomorrow night, right?

Sean finished breading the chicken and then took off his gloves to answer Jasper.

> SEAN: Of course. What time do you want me there?

> JASPER: Trivia starts at seven. How much time do you need to set up?

SEAN: I'll be there by five, you know how I am.

JASPER: Yes, I do, very anal.

SEAN: I'm meticulous.

JASPER: Yes, uptight. You need to get laid. Speaking of, word on the street is you were seen with a woman at Common Grounds.

SEAN: I am in the middle of prepping for our busiest night of the week. I don't have time for this nonsense.

JASPER: Aha! Then it is true, you had a date! When were you going to tell me about it?

SEAN: Nothing to tell.

JASPER: Oh, I beg to differ, my friend. We'll discuss—tomorrow over beers like men do.

SEAN: (man plus beer emoji.)

JASPER: (two beers clinking emoji.)

Sean put his phone back in his pocket and continued prepping. The rest of his staff would be here shortly, and he liked to have a good start on the day by the time they arrived. That meant Mable would show up in about an hour as well, and that didn't give him much time to figure out what he was going to tell her about the date. He wasn't sure how to explain it to himself, let alone answer all the questions he could expect from Mable.

The next hour passed in a moment; this was often the case when Sean got in the prep zone. One moment he was dicing, and the next Mable was banging into his workspace, the door whooshing shut behind her.

"So how did it go?"

"It was nice." He continued slicing tomatoes.

"But?"

"I don't know. It was all going very well. We hung out for hours and we were really connecting, and then all of a sudden she got quiet. Then we left, and she didn't even want me to drive her home." He finished with a sigh.

"You let her walk home?"

Sean's brows lowered, and he leveled a look at Mable, "Of course not."

"So, you drove her home. Good, then what happened?"

"She got out of the Jeep like her hair was on fire, and I haven't heard from her since."

"Did you text her?"

Sean sighed. "Honestly, Mable, I don't see what the point would be."

Mable's mouth dropped. "Wow, I've never seen defeatist Sean before."

"It was one date. We had a good time, but it seems clear she wasn't into me like I was into her. If I'm wrong, the ball is in her court. If I'm right, no good would come from bothering her with a text."

"No, I get it. I think you are making the right call." She patted his shoulder. "I'm sorry it didn't work out."

"Hey, I've still got you, this place, and Hermie."

"The best fish ever!" She laughed.

Chapter Nine

♥

Nicole bustled around her house, changing the towels in the bathroom, making sure a fall candle was lit, and vacuuming for the second time that day. To put it mildly, she had some nervous energy to burn off. Maybe she should try going for a run like Zaina did to combat stress. "That's crazy talk," she said to herself, "You can't stand running." She should probably try to figure out why she was getting all wound up about her friends coming over to hear about the date, but she didn't want to do that.

Her stomach growled. She'd been so flustered she'd never gotten around to eating dinner. Snacks with friends, it would be. She took out a large serving tray and began putting crackers, grapes, cheese, and salami on it. She popped a chunk of aged cheddar cheese in her mouth as she worked and thought about the food Sean had brought to her at the school. Would charcuterie boards make her sad now? "Stop it, Nicole!" she scolded.

Once the food was all set up, Nicole pulled out a bottle of red wine and then checked to make sure there was water ready in the coffeemaker in case anyone wanted decaf or tea. She looked at the clock on her stove; the girls would be here anytime now. She couldn't wait to get this date postmortem over.

Devin took off her coat and threw it, along with her purse, on the recliner next to Nicole's door. She took off her heels and plopped down on the loveseat. "It has been a day," she said, exhausted.

"What's going on, Devin?"

"No ma'am. We are not here to talk about me. We can talk about my mayoral headaches later. Right now, we need to discuss you. What happened? Was he ogling other women while you guys were on your date? Were there red flags? Do I need to sic the health department on him?"

"No, no," she waved her hands urgently, "He's sweet, like a big lovable puppy dog. No red flags! He is going to make some woman a fantastic husband. He'll probably be a great dad too."

"That someone could be you, Nicole," Devin said.

The doorbell rang. "Saved by the bell," Devin quipped, and Nicole opened the door for Zaina.

"Who even rings a doorbell anymore?" Zaina said as she walked in and began unlacing her Doc Martens. Zaina handed Nicole a four-pack of caramel apple hard cider.

Nicole walked over to her kitchen island, "Dev, do you want a cider or red wine?"

"I'll take a glass of wine."

"I'll split a cider with you, Nic," Zaina said.

Nicole poured the drinks, put them on a tray, and walked over to serve her friends.

"You're the best hostess, Nic," said Devin.

Zaina took a small plate and loaded it with charcuterie. "I ate right before I came over, but I can't resist cheese. I think it's my main character flaw," she joked.

Devin said, "Cheese doesn't love me. Thank goodness for Lactaid." She made herself a plate and sat back with her glass of wine. "Come sit down, Nicole." She patted the seat next to her. "It's not an interrogation. I promise."

"Cool, cool," Nicole said, "By the way, how is Ben?"

Devin shook her finger back and forth. "Ah-ah-ah, we are not going off on a tangent about Ben. He's at home enjoying some quality time with his children. He's heading out of town for a week tomorrow."

Nicole turned to Zaina. "How's Mike?"

"You guys, I think he is going to propo—"

Devin shot Zaina the same look she used on the twins when they misbehaved. Unlike the twins, Zaina complied immediately.

"Never mind," Zaina smiled sweetly. "Tell us about the date, Nic."

An hour and a half later, the drinks were gone, tears and laughter had been shed, and Nicole was ready to receive any advice her friends could give.

Devin gave Zaina a nod. "You go first," she said.

"I guess the big question is, are you ready?"

"When you say ready, what exactly do you mean?" Nicole asked.

Devin huffed and couldn't stop herself from jumping in to explain. "She's asking if you want a relationship! Because if you do, we can get you a second chance with Sean."

"Then yes, I am ready. I feel more nauseous at the thought of not trying than the thought of talking to Sean again."

Devin and Zaina high-fived.

"Should I text him?" Nicole asked. "It's only nine-thirty. I could text him now?"

"Definitely not," said Zaina at the same time Devin said, "No way, too easy to ignore."

"We know he's going to be at the brewery's trivia night tomorrow, so you and I can go there. If you're in, we can plan your outfit now. Then when he sees you his eyes will fall out of his head, and you just ask him out," Zaina said.

Devin nodded in agreement. "Piece. Of. Cake," she punctuated each word with a nail tap on the table.

Nicole cocked her head to the side. She didn't think it would be a piece of cake, but she was ready to try. "I do have a cute new wrap shirt."

Devin made a bring it motion. "Let's see it, and I know you don't do heels, but it's cool enough for boots. How about dark wash jeans tucked into knee-high black boots?"

"I can do that."

Zaina clapped her hands. "Yes! And what about straightening your hair?"

"No," Devin said. "Soft curls, do you have a curling iron?"

Nicole nodded, "I don't think I've used it in at least five years, but yes."

"What I'm thinking is some curls and then," she walked over to Nicole and started playing with her hair. "Just pull a little bit back here with a clip or some bobby pins; then you'll have it off your gorgeous face and some curls will frame it. Add on dangling earrings and let a little peek of the girls out in that shirt and he will be in your thrall."

Nicole turned and pulled both Zaina and Devin into a hug.

"Group hug, girls!" They all hugged, and Nicole continued, "I never want to know what I'd do without you two."

"Love you, Nic," said Zaina.

"You got this," Devin said. "I only wish I could be there to see it. Make sure you take a video, Zaina."

"I got you," Zaina said.

Chapter Ten

♥

Sean was feeling good as he opened the railroad car that was used as the outdoor bar and grill at Hop's Heaven. It was a gorgeous evening just before the official start of fall. Temps had fallen from the mid-eighties to a very comfortable seventy-five degrees, a perfect night to be under the Oktoberfest tent for trivia night. He was confident his appetizer menu was going to be a huge hit.

Jasper came out to the rail car and gave Sean a half hug and a smack on the back. "Buddy, long time no see!"

"Jasp, thanks again for having me out."

"Hey, you're helping me out! Whenever we have appetizers, or any food from Jesse's Pub, people stay longer and drink more. Plus, it brings out the ladies. Sometimes it's a real boys' club around here, and that's not my thing."

"Jasp, you're such a slut. Are you ever not looking to score?" Sean chided.

"I'm young, good-looking and single. Why wouldn't I hook up with—I mean get to know—as many women as possible." Jasper ran a hand through his thick, wavy brown hair, which he wore long enough to hit his shoulders. "The other day, a patron thought I was twenty-eight. She said I had rakish good looks."

"Was it that writer? The one who reminds me of my Aunt Sarah?"

"Hilarious. She's a very young sixty. Let me tell you, she knows handsome men when she sees them. I tell you what, she writes filthy dirty romance books. Your eyes would fall out of your head if you read some of the smut she's published." Jasper shook his head from side to side. "She may look like a sweet little grandma, but it's all an act."

"I'll take your word for it, bud." Sean busied himself setting up the serving trays and Sterno cans for the evening.

Jasper sat at the counter. "So what do we have here?"

"I went with the classics. We have red cabbage with caraway seeds, bratwurst sliders on pretzel buns with a spicy brown mustard, German twice-baked baby potatoes, and mini apple and pumpkin tarts."

"Damn, I asked for appetizers, and you came with a full-on meal!"

"Well, the portions are small. It's more like autumn tapas." Sean made Jasper a plate.

Jasper came around the bar to pour himself a Marley Creek Marzen. "Can I get you one too?"

"Just a few ounces, or I'll fall asleep on my feet. I slept like crap last night."

"That sucks. Or did your date the other night tire you out? I haven't forgotten about that. You were going to tell me what happened. How'd it go?"

Sean took the beer that Jasper offered and drank a sip. "Ah, that's an excellent beer! You've done it again, Jasper."

"Thanks, bud."

"Try it with the slider. It will pair well together."

They both took a drink of beer and a bite of their sandwiches. "Ahh," they both said and fist-bumped.

"Now back to the date. What's her name?"

"Nicole Garrett."

"Nicole Garrett," Jasper said, thinking, "Yes, Nicki. He snapped his fingers. Yeah, we went to high school together. I think she was in my math class, or maybe it was biology? Nice girl, quiet. We ran in different circles, but I'd probably recognize her if I saw her. She must still live around here, huh?"

"Yep, she lives right by Jesse's."

"Hey, that'll be handy. You can head over to her place after a long day behind the stove. She can help you relax." Jasper waggled his eyebrows suggestively.

Sean just rolled his eyes. "I don't think anything like that is going to happen. Everything was going great; we were there talking and laughing. We lost track of time, and you know how you feel that spark, that chemistry?"

"Sexual tension?"

"Yes, it was there! I know she felt it too! God, it was so disappointing."

"Did you come on too strong? Please tell me you didn't start sharing your life plan. Did you tell her how you don't see yourself having kids and how what you want most out of a relationship is someone to be your partner for life? Was the word soulmate part of the conversation?"

"First of all, no. And second of all—," Sean punched Jasper in the arm.

"What was that for?" he yelped.

"You being ridiculous. I don't know what happened! Everything was going great and then all of a sudden, she just went cold. Then we left, and I drove her home. She could not have gotten out of the car any faster; she practically opened the door and rolled out while I was pulling into her driveway!"

Jasper was mid-swallow when he started laughing so hard that beer went up his nose. He kept laughing until there were tears streaming down his face, and Sean had joined in as well.

"I-I c-can't stop picturing it! Her rolling out of your Jeep," Jasper gasped.

"I'll admit; it's pretty funny, but damn it, I liked her. I thought maybe...well, at least I thought we'd go out again. See, this is why I haven't been dating. I'm not built for the on-again, off-again."

"Oh, I know, Sean. You are, ah, like a golden retriever."

"I'm a dog?"

"I mean not in a bad way, more like the opposite. You're easy-going and you are the most reliable friend I have. And you're a hugger. See, like a golden retriever."

Sean rocked his head from side to side. "Okay, I see what you mean. I don't hate it. I suppose I am like that. Too bad you weren't there, then you could tell me what Nicole is. She's definitely not a golden retriever."

"Well, maybe she's had a bad break up or two? Or maybe she just wasn't into you?" Jasper leaned back and tapped a finger on his lips. "You want to know what I would do?"

"I know what you'd do. You'd just move on. Plenty of fish in the sea, tons of honeys waiting for you on the app."

Jasper screwed up his face, "Tons of honeys, what does that even mean? You're a riot, Sean. That's why I keep you around;

you make me laugh and you are the best chef. What I was going to say was, if you think there was something there, what could it hurt to send her a text? If she leaves you on read, you'll know she's not interested; if she replies, you just go from there. I think you are overthinking it. Women aren't that complicated."

And with that, Jasper got up and headed back inside the main brewery building.

***

Nicole was scrolling social media, trying to distract herself until it was time for Zaina to pick her up. Usually watching random stranger's videos online made time fly. Today the minutes were creeping by. She shouldn't have gotten ready so early. Now all she could do was sit and hope her hair stayed sexy. She put down her phone and went back to the bathroom to check her makeup and hair. She gently fluffed the curls around her face and adjusted the clip in her hair.

Devin was a marvel at hair and makeup. Nicole didn't know how she always looked so put together, especially since she had twins to chase after. Not to mention, she was always running around between her law office and being mayor. Nicole recalled Devin saying her mom had drilled into her the importance of always looking proper. "Black women don't get the same consideration your white friends might get. You always have to be on point in your clothing, hair and manners."

Nicole had always been a wash-and-go girl, except for the bad days. She looked in the mirror once again, admiring her hair. Thank God it had grown back. Losing her hair during chemo had not only ached as it happened, but once it was gone, she couldn't hide that she was sick. She couldn't go anywhere without strangers knowing she had cancer, and she hated that. Nicole took a deep breath and pushed those emotions away. She should be excited about where she was now; dwelling in the past, wishing she'd never had to deal with cancer wasn't living. Once she started thinking about the bad old days, it was hard for her to stop.

She thought back to when she'd been at her lowest, going for weekly chemo treatments. All those Thursdays sitting in the infusion room with Zaina or Devin by her side and talking about all the things she was going to do when she was done fighting cancer. It had been so easy to talk about the wonderful life she was going to have, the wonderful life she was supposed to be living right now.

Somehow, she'd become trapped in a comfort zone of work, sensible eating, moderate exercise and avoiding as much stress as possible, all to guarantee the cancer never came back. She thought that maybe if she just kept her head down and didn't make any waves, the universe would reward her with a long life and no cancer ever again. She knew it wasn't logical, but that's how she lived, and it had been working just fine for her. What would her old self say, the one to whom she'd made promises to about living life? Her head was full of so many conflicting thoughts she began to convince herself she'd be better off if she just stayed home tonight.

Her phone chimed. Too late now, Zaina was here. She put her purse over her shoulder and made sure she had her house keys, then she hustled out the door to Zaina's waiting car. Nicole got in and put her seatbelt on.

"You look amazing," Zaina said as she backed out of Nicole's driveway.

Nicole did a double take as she took in Zaina's hair. She had on an ombre blonde to light pink shoulder-length bob. It was quite a change from her usual platinum blonde pixie cut, but with Zaina's delicate features and petite frame, she could pull off almost any hairstyle or outfit.

"What's with the new look?"

"You like it? I figured I'd try it out tonight. I got it for the Chamber's Witches Night Out for Breast Cancer Awareness that's coming up in a few weeks. You're coming, right?"

Nicole frowned. "Honestly, that rah! rah!" she made air quotes, "you'll beat it, you're a warrior, pink stuff — I find it annoying."

"How come?" Zaina asked. "I thought you of all people would be pro-breast cancer awareness."

"I'm all too aware," she laughed ironically. "It's not that I'm against it in principle. It's because I know all too well that for many people, men and women, their cancer isn't early stage and they don't get a do-over. They have it and then they die."

Zaina was quiet for a moment before responding, "I hear you. I guess I don't think about that part of it. I'm too focused on the fun and celebrating survivors."

The only sound in the car was the quiet hum of the motor. "I'm sorry. I didn't mean to be a downer," Nicole whispered.

"Don't apologize. It's good for me to hear this. I'm on the planning committee for the event. What could we do to make it less frustrating for people like you, especially survivors and their families?"

Nicole had an answer ready because she had been thinking about the dreaded October Breast Cancer Awareness campaigns. "Give some of the money to groups that help people with stage four breast cancer. But it still needs to be a fun event, and people who are happy are more likely to give money, right?"

"True," said Zaina. "Do you think you have time to help me put something together for the committee?"

Nicole felt lighter; a little of the weight she carried these days had lifted. Maybe if she talked about some of the cancer baggage she carried with people she loved, she'd feel better. "I'd love to help!"

On that high note, Zaina put her hybrid in park, and they got out and walked into Hop's Heaven.

Zaina led the way up to the bar. "Hi!" she said brightly to the bartender. They wore their hair in a long red braid and had arm sleeve tattoos.

Nicole recognized that one sleeve comprised Pokémon characters, and the other looked like it was all Marvel heroes. "Nice tattoos," she said. "I like your Bulbasaur."

The bartender nodded. "Thanks," they said. "What can I get you?"

"What's a Bobasar?"

Nicole rolled her eyes dramatically. "That's a Bulbasaur. It's a Pokémon character. It's the one that looks like some kind of frog or turtle with spots and has like a sack on its back."

Zaina looked at the bartender's arm. "Okay, I see that. Since when do you know about Pokémon characters?"

"I know way too many things that are popular with small children. The kids at school love all things Pokémon, and after fifteen years, I've picked up a few things."

"That makes sense," Zaina said and then added. "While you were talking about kids' toys, I found out we need to go outside for the trivia night. That's where it takes place and apparently there's a hot chef selling a-mazing food and we have to try the German potato bites." Zaina gestured over her shoulder. "Or at least that's what that lady over there told me."

Nicole's stomach flip-flopped; it was time to put up or shut up, as they said. Panicked, she clutched Zaina's hand. "I don't think I can do this!" she hissed.

Zaina took Nicole's other hand and looked her in the eyes. "You look stunning. You said he's a decent guy, right?"

Nicole nodded.

"Why wouldn't he want to go out with you again if you approached him? He'd be crazy not to! You are going to walk up to him, and he is going to be stunned into silence by your beauty. Then you are going to ask him out and he is just going to nod his head and say anytime, anywhere. You've got this!"

"I've got this," Nicole squared her shoulders.

"It's going to be fun!"

"It's not going to be fun."

Zaina wrapped her arm around her friend, "It will be if you let it."

Nicole put her head on Zaina's shoulder for a moment and then stepped back, ready to head outside and see Sean.

***

He was refreshing the bratwurst slider tray when she walked into the tent. A light breeze was blowing, and it tousled her hair as she sauntered his way. He barely noticed the fact that he'd loosened his grip on the tongs he was using to hold a slider. It fell to the ground as he visibly gulped, taking in her slim waist and the curves of her hips. He imagined pulling on the tie that held her wrap shirt in place. One pull and those soft breasts nestled in a lacy black bra would be his to lavish with attention. He shifted as his jeans grew uncomfortable with his growing arousal. Fortunately, he was behind the bar, and she'd never know.

She made eye contact with him and smiled a soft smile. He bit his bottom lip in an effort to contain himself. *Why was she there?* She closed the gap and was suddenly leaning on the counter in front of him. Sean wanted to lean over and kiss her supple lips. Suddenly he was picturing himself reaching over and brushing the back of his hand against her cheek and then gripping her face lightly. He imagined bending down and kissing her, at first gently and then hard and fast as he slid his hands down to her waist and pulled her to him.

"Fancy meeting you here," he said to break the hold his daydream had on him, hoping to relieve some of the pressure of his zipper rubbing against his cock.

"Hi Sean," she said so softly he could barely hear her over the music playing and the noise of the gathering crowd. He gestured one second with his finger and walked away from the buffet to the end of the bar where she stood.

"Sorry about that. I couldn't hear you." He put his arms on the bar and leaned into her space. He could smell that delicious vanilla and jasmine scent of hers.

"I'm here with my friend, Zaina." She pointed to where Zaina was drinking a beer and laughing as the guy running the trivia night handed her a paper.

"Do you usually come to trivia night? Gad, that sounds like a cheesy pick up line. I didn't mean it to sound like I was saying, Hey, there pretty lady, come here often?" He said in an over-the-top tone.

"Oh, no." She shook her head, and he delighted in the way the curls bounced around her heart-shaped face. "I didn't think that at all, and no, I've never come to trivia night. I've only been to Hop's Heaven once or twice."

"Gotcha," he said nodding, his chest fluttering with hope. He clenched his fist to stop himself, but he had to know. He blurted out, "So, why did you come here?"

Her cheeks burned red, and he felt like a fool.

"I came here for you." She said simply and put a hand on his arm, and static electricity shocked them both. They jumped back and laughed nervously. Then Nicole was looking at him again, and all he saw was her longing.

"Why me?" Sean asked softly.

"I'm here to apologize for coming off so disinterested at the end of our date. It was not you; it was all me. And I'm sorry. I was a total jerk."

"Apology accepted," he blurted.

She smiled widely and then looked down. "I was hoping," she looked up and met his eyes, "we might go out again?"

Internally, Sean was doing a happy dance and high fiving all the voices in his head. Externally, he tried to play it cool, nodding slowly. "I would be down for that," he said. "What did you have in mind?"

"I know you have to run the restaurant, and I'm sure the last thing you'd like to do is to go out for a late dinner—"

"I have a hard time turning off my restaurateur brain at other places, so yes, that's exactly right."

"Monday is parent-teacher conference day, so I don't go into work until two. I was thinking we could go to Marley Lake for a walk, and I can bring a picnic lunch for us?"

Sean smiled, and his dimples flashed. "I love it; it's a date."

Nicole hopped up and gave him a half-hug over the counter. Sean restrained himself from pulling her up and over the bar and into his arms. She smelled so good.

"I can be ready by eleven. Would you like me to pick you up?"

"Nah, I can drive. It's a date then?" Sean confirmed.

"I'm so excited!" Nicole exclaimed.

"Me too," he said, and he winked at her.

She gave him a little wave and walked over to where her friend with the pink wig was sitting. Her friend looked familiar, but Sean wasn't sure where he'd seen her before.

Chapter Eleven

♥

The last few days had flown by, and the best part of her days had been the text exchange she'd been having with Sean. Light, flirty fun texts, nothing serious, no drama. She loved the lack of drama most of all. She'd be happy to stay in this anticipatory zone forever. But today was the day, and even though she was closer to forty than fourteen, she felt like a teenager going out with a boy she'd had a crush on. She didn't mind it. It felt good, this feeling of a new beginning.

Nicole looked in the mirror and smiled at the light in her eyes. She put on lip gloss in the hopes that perhaps Sean would kiss it off later. She did a little shimmy dance and walked over to her turntable to put on an old record. "Who even am I?" she said out loud. "Here I am packing a freaking picnic basket to go on a lunch date. Life is wild!" She pulled out Swiss and cheddar cheese, as well as ham and turkey deli meat, and placed them on the counter. She opened the twelve-grain bread she'd bought yesterday and began making a couple of sandwiches.

When she'd told Devin about her picnic date, Devin had offered her picnic basket. It was embossed with her and Ben's initials. She said they'd gotten it as a wedding present, and it had been sitting in their basement since before the twins were born because they weren't picnic people. Nicole figured today she'd discover if she and Sean were picnic people.

Her phone buzzed with a text notification. It was Devin.

> DEV: Do you have a few minutes? I need to vent? Call me?

Nicole turned off her record player and put in her headphones to call Devin.

"Hi Dev, what's up?"

"Thanks for calling me, Nic. I've got to vent to someone, or my head might explode, and Ben is en route to Wichita again. I'm in the car driving so I've got you on speakerphone, but no one is in the car with me."

"Thanks. You know how I hate being on speakerphone. Sean isn't picking me up for another twenty minutes, so vent away."

"Am I bothering you while you're trying to get ready?"

"Not at all. I've been ready since like nine a.m."

"Hon, I'm so happy for you!"

"It's just a lunch date."

"Yes, but this is huge for you."

Nicole blushed. "I'm trying. Now vent away."

"It's that damn Oktoberfest. Not only are residents complaining, now the guys in public works are blowing a gasket. There have already been more complaints so far this year than all of last year, and we still have weeks to go."

"As far as the residents go, could it be that one person is making most of the calls? Do we have an old crank that doesn't want anyone to have any fun?"

"Sadly, no, they aren't repeat complainers, and even worse, the police have arrested five people so far for drunk and disorderly conduct! This has never happened before. I've even got Midwest Metra complaining about people acting up on the train. I don't know what's going on."

"I had no clue! Do you have any idea why this is happening?"

"No, I'm not sure why this year is out of hand, but this can't continue. I know the business community enjoys the bump Oktoberfest gives them, but this town can't afford the disruption or the cost of increased policing and OT for public works. We are out of funds and I'm out of patience. The peace and safety of Marley Creek residents is my primary concern."

"What are you going to do?"

"I don't know yet. The town council meets next Tuesday. We'll be looking at existing ordinances and considering a new ordinance that would make it illegal to have a large-scale event for more than two days without unanimous approval of the town council."

"Wow, that would have a huge impact on small businesses like Zaina's and Sean's."

"I hear you, but they would still have the Mistletoe Market and the summer tourists. I mean this is only the third year for Oktoberfest. It's not like it's an institution like our marathon, and if it is causing major disruption to our town, it's my job to look out for the citizens even if that causes some short-term distress to our business community."

"No, no, I get it. I understand where you are coming from. Your job is to keep our town safe. If Oktoberfest is a problem, then you've got to look at shutting it down."

"Thanks for being my sounding board. I appreciate you."

"Anytime, Dev, that's what we do for each other. I don't want to imagine a world where I don't have you and Zaina to talk me out of my worst mistakes."

"Same. Okay, I'll let you go. Have fun on your date with your man!"

"He's not my man...yet." Nicole smiled a sly smile.

"That's my girl! I think you are back!"

"Love you," Nicole said, her heart full.

"To the moon," Devin said and ended the call.

Nicole checked her watch. Only a few more minutes until Sean arrived. She could hardly contain herself. She felt like she'd just guzzled a thirty-two-ounce energy drink. Speaking of drinks, she walked over to the fridge and added a couple bottles of water to the basket. She hoped Sean wouldn't be expecting wine with their lunch since she had to go to work right after.

The doorbell rang, and she ran to the door. She took a quick look in the peephole just to make sure it wasn't UPS delivering a package. She paused before she opened the door to take a quick glance in the mirror and smooth her wavy hair.

***

"Hey, you," Sean said as he took in Nicole. His eyes went straight to her glossy lips. He wanted to know if her lip gloss was flavored, and he made a promise that by the end of this date he'd taste it for himself. "These are for you," he said and handed her a bouquet of zinnias and sunflowers wrapped in butcher paper and tied with twine.

"Oh my gosh! Thank you so much. They are beautiful. Where did you get them? Don't tell me, are these from your garden?"

"I'd love to take credit for them, but I picked them up from Lucy's Flower Shop."

"They are so vibrant. Thank you again." She leaned over and kissed him on the cheek. He was sorely tempted to put his arms around her and kiss her properly, but he told himself, *You've got to take it* slow. *Sean*. He knew he needed to let her set the pace. There was no hurry; they could take their time and maybe, just maybe, they'd have a lifetime to spend together. It seemed crazy that he was thinking long term, before they'd even had an actual date, but it felt right to him. He watched her walk into the kitchen to put the flowers in a vase and admired the way her jeans accented her pert ass. *All in good time*, he told his libido.

While she was taking care of the flowers and getting the picnic basket, he looked around her space. Her house was a small ranch with an open floor plan so he could see the kitchen and the living room from where he stood. The floors were well-worn wood with a few colorful scattered throw rugs. A large picture window was next to the front door, and in front of it there was a wooden plant stand filled with houseplants, including a philodendron, a jade plant, and a begonia. Her house faced south, and the plants showed it. They were flourishing.

Past the planter was the main sitting area with a comfortable-looking recliner and a large overstuffed loveseat In front of that was a long coffee table that looked like it was made with a single large piece of wood. She placed the vase with his flowers on it. Across the room from the sitting area was a fireplace. On the mantle, he could see pictures of what he assumed were family and friends, but he didn't want to go up to the pictures and start asking questions. On each side of the fireplace were built-in bookshelves, and they were packed with books. He couldn't remember dating anyone, possibly ever, who had bookcases filled with books.

Everything about Nicole's place suited her, and he felt at ease being in her home. Her place was cozy and made him feel like he was in a cabin out in the woods. He started daydreaming about what it would be like to come home to Nicole and this house after a long day at Jesse's Pub. He could see himself relaxing in the recliner while a fire crackled and Nicole sat on the love seat curled up with a good book and a nice cup of chai.

She thrust the picnic basket into his hands and broke up his daydream. "Ready to go? I've got to be back to go to work by one-thirty or one forty-five at the very latest."

"Then we better get going," he said. He walked outside and stowed the picnic basket in the back of his Jeep, then he went around to hold the door for Nicole. She climbed into the passenger seat. He walked around to the driver's side, got in, and they were off.

"I'm so glad we got such a nice day," Nicole said cheerfully, the sun shining on her face, bringing out the gold highlights in her reddish-brown hair.

"I realize how corny this sounds, but even if it were pouring rain, I'd be happy to spend some time with you."

"It's ridiculously corny, and I feel exactly the same."

He took one hand off the steering wheel and placed it palm up on her armrest. She reached over and held his hand as they drove to Marley Lake.

The weather was warm for late September, with temperatures in the low seventies, so Sean found a pleasant spot of grass, and Nicole spread the blanket and unpacked the lunch. He helped by making their plates, and soon they were eating. They were both hungry and ate the fresh sandwiches and potato salad that Nicole had prepared in a companionable quiet. Sean marveled at how relaxed he felt with Nicole. Unlike other dates he'd been on in the past few years, he didn't feel any pressure to make conversation as they finished lunch.

"Well, I'm stuffed," Sean said, patting his stomach. "My compliments to the chef."

"You are too kind," Nicole said and flipped her hair.

"Let me pack everything up and then we can just hang out for a bit, okay?"

"That sounds wonderful." She stretched out her legs and leaned back on her arms. She looked out on the lake, and he watched her for a moment, warmth spreading through his chest.

Once the debris from their lunch was put away, Sean moved next to Nicole and put an arm around her shoulders. "This is nice," she said.

"How much time do we have?" Sean asked.

She glanced at her phone and said, "About twenty minutes." She put down her phone and turned toward him. He leaned down, and she closed her eyes.

"Can I?" he asked, and she answered before he could finish speaking.

"Yes, please. Please kiss me," she said breathy, and he leaned in and gently touched his lips to the lips he'd been dreaming about kissing for days. He kissed her slowly, then bit tenderly on her lower lip. She moaned softly and he slid his tongue out, opening her lips, and soon their tongues were entwined. He pulled her onto his lap, and she ran her hands through his hair. They came up for air when the alarm started going off on her phone. She scrambled off him, and he missed the warmth of her.

She straightened her shirt, and he waited a moment to stand up. Then he pulled her into a hug and kissed her forehead. "Better get you to work," he said. She wrapped an arm around his waist and stood on her tiptoes to steal a kiss. Then she pulled up the blanket and folded it while he picked up the picnic basket, and they headed to his Jeep.

He turned on the radio when they got in the car, and she began humming along. She wasn't singing, but he could tell she'd have a lovely voice. Hopefully, he would hear her sing—soon, in the shower after they had mind-blowing sex.

Chapter Twelve

♥

Zaina threw her arms around Nicole. "Thanks for coming by tonight. I was just getting ready to close."

Nicole raised a takeout bag. "I brought dessert. It's caramel apple cheesecake."

"I'm starving. We were busy tonight, and I didn't have time to eat. I can't believe I forgot my work snack bag at home. The closer we get to October, the busier I get. Lots of my regulars were in tonight. It's almost time for the Harvest Moon."

"Yes, that's always a big day for your coven, isn't it?" Nicole joked.

"Hilarious! If I had a coven, it wouldn't be complete without you and Devin."

"Good to know."

"Do you want a cup of tea to go with our dessert, or water?"

"I'll just take water. It's hot out there," Nicole fanned herself.

"It's still so summery out that people aren't thinking fall yet. I haven't sold any of the new shirts yet, and I've got sweaters coming in any day now. Who wants a sweater when it's eighty degrees outside?"

"It'll cool off as it always does, and then all your witchy stuff will fly off the shelves." Nicole unpacked the two slices of cheesecake, napkins, and forks.

Zania brought over water for both of them and sat down. She looked at her friend Nicole quizzically. "You're in quite a good mood. How's your man?"

Nicole blushed. "He's not my man."

"Isn't he, though?"

Nicole's face was red hot now. "We've only gone out a couple of times. It's been like a week."

"Whatever. I have a good feeling about you two. I don't need the cards to tell me you're happy, and Sean seems to be a really good guy. The only flaw I've seen is he has questionable taste in friends." Zania commented.

"Right, Jasper."

"Ugh, don't even say his name." She put her hands over her ears. "I can't stand that guy."

"Well, then you should be happy to hear that Devin is saying they are having so many problems with his Oktoberfest that the town council might shut it down."

Zania froze, her fork halfway to her mouth. She put it down and said, "Oh no, no, no, that can't happen!"

"What's wrong? I thought you hated Jasper and only wished bad things for him. Didn't you used to stick pins in a poppet Jasper?"

Zania waved her hands. "It's not that; it's Oktoberfest! Do you realize how many sales I make on the weekends thanks to all the people who come in to go to Hop's Heaven? Oktoberfest helps keep me afloat during the winter! Plus, I've already paid for a bunch of inventory for the next few weekends. And not only that, I've got vendors bringing me stuff on consignment. Oktoberfest doesn't just help Jasper, which of course I don't care about. It helps me and all the teeny tiny vendors I've invited to display their fall and Samhain themed crafts. This can't happen!" Zania's face crumbled.

Nicole rubbed her friend's back, "I had no idea how important Oktoberfest was for you."

"Not just me! Oktoberfest has been helping all of us over the past few years! Did you know Books and Breads supplies all the pretzels for Oktoberfest? Last year, they sold over ten-thousand dollars in giant pretzels."

"Wow," Nicole said. "Maybe we can talk to Devin? Get her to work with Jasper?"

Zaina crossed her arms and leveled a look at her friend.

"C'mon, you know we can't do that. We promised we'd keep our friendship separate from Devin's job as mayor and never try to use our personal relationship to influence her. We pinky promised."

Nicole nodded her head, "Crap! I totally forgot about the promise! Okay, so we can't do that, but maybe there's a way we can work with Jasper to keep Oktoberfest going and reduce the bad behavior of some of the guests."

They both sat in silence for a minute, thinking. Zaina's face was blotchy with stress, and Nicole played with her hair absently while she tried to think of a way to fix things. Then Nicole spoke up, "Maybe I can talk to Sean? Explain how serious the situation is and ask him to get Jasper on board to fix things."

"Would you? Do you think Sean can get Jasper to see the light?"

"I think if anyone around here can, it's Sean. He was telling me about when he first arrived in Marley Creek. Did you know he interned at Jasper's place before he opened Jesse's Pub?"

"I had no idea."

"Not only did he intern for him, that summer Sean lived with Jasper, and they became super close."

Zaina nodded, "Makes sense."

"Sean was telling me about some of their adventures that summer. He mentioned that for Jasper, Hop's Heaven isn't just his livelihood; it's his identity. He may seem like a casual guy who's always dating at least one girl who looks like a model, and he plays like he doesn't keep track of every sale made at the brewery. But the reality is he's obsessed with making a name for himself in the craft brewery space. His goal is to franchise Hop's Heaven."

"Then it's got to work; he has too much riding on this to let it get canceled."

"I know you haven't been able to stand Jasper since high school, but do you think you could put that aside and maybe you could go talk to him too?"

"Oh, goddess, no," Zaina said abruptly.

"Okay, okay, I'll talk to Sean. Maybe you could think about talking to Jasper, just in case, if it would make a difference?"

"I don't see how I could talk sense into Jasper."

"You're probably right," Nicole said, sensing she shouldn't try to push Zaina further.

Zaina went back to eating her cheesecake then piped up, "I have an idea."

"Let's hear it."

"It sounds like Hop's Heaven needs extra help and some good PR in the town."

"For sure," Nicole nodded.

"So maybe I can talk to some of the other shop owners, you know, people who are benefiting from Oktoberfest, like Donnie over at Books and Breads, and we could help serve in the tent. We'd work to help defray the cost of extra security, and it would show that the local business community will do what it takes to keep Oktoberfest around. If we all pitched in, then Oktoberfest won't seem like it's just a brewery event. I'll post about the problems Oktoberfest is having in our Marley Creek Business Group and see other solutions the group can come up with to make Oktoberfest a community-focused event and not a big boozy fest that bothers the neighborhood."

"That sounds genius, Zaina. I'm sure that Jasper will go for that if you can get the support from other businesses."

"We've got to save Oktoberfest. Some of these businesses won't survive without it. Heck, I would barely make it! The Mistletoe Market used to be the only chance I had to stay out of the red, but when Oktoberfest came around, I've had some room to breathe the last couple years. Do you know what a relief that is for me?"

Nicole squeezed her friend's hand. "We are going to do this, I promise you."

***

Sean was lying down on his couch, too tired to get up and brush his teeth and go to bed when his phone started ringing.

"Hey baby," Nicole said. "Did you have a good Saturday?"

Sean loved it when Nicole called him 'baby'. It was so out of character for her. She wasn't a nickname or call people pet names kind of woman.

"My feet are killing me, and we sold out of all the bratwurst I had for the week."

"Why don't you come over and I can massage your feet," she offered.

"Darling, I'd love to, but I'm so tired I'd fall asleep on the drive over."

"Want me to let you go?"

"No, not yet. I want to hear about your day. If I start snoring, just hang up."

She giggled, and he pictured her in bed. He was tempted to ask her what she was wearing, but he didn't want to push things. They'd only gone out a couple of times, and he didn't want to scare her off. He wondered though, did she sleep in long T-shirts, or a tank top and undies? Or maybe she didn't sleep in anything at all? He couldn't wait to find out.

"So, tell me about your day."

"It was your basic errands day, not much to talk about until I went over to Zaina's."

"Tell me again. Who's Zaina?"

"She's my oldest friend in the world. Umm, oh yeah, she was with me at trivia night. She's tiny."

"To be honest, I wasn't paying attention to anyone but you that night."

"Aww, every time I think I can't like you more, you say something like that, and it's not BS. You're sincere! I'm not used to this."

Get used to it, *darling.* "When you're in the room, well, I only have eyes for you."

"Thank you," she whispered, her voice deep with emotion. "Zania is the one that owns New Age Stones & Witch Crafts. She had on a pink wig."

"Gotcha. She looked familiar, but I couldn't place her. Maybe I've seen her at a Chamber of Commerce meeting or something."

"Probably. She's pretty involved in the Marley Creek business community, and that segues right into something I need your help with."

"Whatever it is, I'm happy to help however I can."

"I'm glad to hear you say that. I love your can-do spirit and I'm not sure how else to approach this problem," she said seriously. Then she told Sean all about the problems Devin had shared because of Oktoberfest, as well as how much of an impact it had on Zaina's business and all the other brick-and-mortar stores on Main Street. He listened and asked questions as she spoke. His mind was whirling; Jasper sometimes kept his nose so close to the grindstone that he didn't realize when he was focused on the wrong things.

"Nicole, I think you and Zaina have a good idea here. I'll talk to Jasper and I'm sure he'll want to do whatever he can to keep Oktoberfest going. How much time do you think we have to turn this around?"

"I don't think there is much time at all. I know the town council has a meeting coming up on Tuesday. Any chance you can talk Jasper into going to the meeting? I know there's time for public comments. Oh shoot, I know we had plans on Tuesday, but—"

"No, you're right. This is more important right now. We can go to the movies another time; although, just to be clear, I'd much rather be sharing one of those big movie theater recliners and a bucket of popcorn with you than to be sitting in the town hall listening to people complaining."

"How about after the meeting, you come over and we'll watch a movie here? I don't have a recliner for two, but I do have a loveseat and microwave popcorn."

"That sounds even better than our original plan."

"Maybe I'll even massage your feet."

"I'm going to hold you to that." Sean looked down at his sore feet and wondered if he could fit in a pedicure before Tuesday. He was all for a foot massage, but he also wanted to have presentable feet the first time Nicole saw them. He yawned into the phone before he could stop himself.

"You sound exhausted. I'll let you go. Get some sleep."

"Now that I've talked to you, I can go to sleep happy."

"Sweet dreams, Sean."

"Right back at you."

They ended their call. Sean thought about taking the time to text Jasper right away, but his eyes were barely staying open. So, he dragged himself to the bathroom, where he brushed his teeth and cleaned his face. Then he put his phone on the charger and climbed into bed. He'd talk to Jasper tomorrow night.

Chapter Thirteen

As soon as Nicole got home from work on Tuesday, she FaceTimed Zaina to check-in. "Are you ready for tonight?" Nicole asked Zaina.

"Just my business on the line. No big deal. Hopefully, we've got this, and the worst part will be having to be in a room with that obnoxious ass Jasper."

"Ah, you'll be fine, just stick with me."

"Sure, but you'll be with Sean, and he'll be with Jasper."

Nicole rolled her eyes. "I wanted to run this past you. I was thinking one of us should give Devin a heads up about us being at the meeting and that Jasper will be coming to speak. I don't want her to feel blindsided by us."

"I think that's the right call. I know we promised not to use our friendship in any way that could look like we were asking for favors from her, but this is different."

"Exactly my thoughts. I'll call her because I don't have a dog in this fight and that way, she'll know and whatever happens at the meeting happens."

Zaina's shop bell rang. "I gotta go. Customer just walked in," and she ended the call.

Nicole changed out of her work clothes and looked through her closet for an outfit that worked for the meeting and also for her date with Sean. Even though they'd be staying in, she wanted to look nice. Her heart began to race, and she realized that while she hadn't invited him to spend the night, he might expect to take the next step. Overwhelmed, she plopped down on her bed.

She didn't know if she was ready for sex. She hadn't been with anyone since her and Duncan started dating, and that had been nearly seven years ago. More importantly, she hadn't been with anyone since she'd had surgery, and the thought of taking off her clothes in front of someone, well, just taking off her shirt, made her light-headed. She wrapped her arms across her stomach in response to the thought of being exposed.

She liked Sean, and it wasn't like she didn't fantasize about him naked in her bed, but she was afraid of what he would think when her clothes came off. When she had had surgery, her only thought was getting the cancer out. She didn't think about the future, and she *never* thought about how one day she might want to take off her top and bra in front of someone she was dating. Maybe she could always keep them on. She rolled her eyes at herself, but when she thought about sex with Sean, keeping her shirt on made her feel safe.

Having decided on a plan, Nicole went back into her closet and found a soft T-shirt with a little V-neck, nothing too deep. She changed out of the button-down blouse she'd planned to wear. Then she adjusted the padded insert in her bra that made her look even and pulled her grey T-shirt over her head. Then she added an olive and cream crochet cardigan and checked her look in the mirror. She felt comfortable and looked put-together for the meeting.

Nicole sat down at her kitchen table and called Devin. She answered on the second ring.

"Hi Devin, it's Nicole. Am I interrupting anything?"

"If you were, I wouldn't have answered the phone. You know me," Devin chuckled.

"I know that there have been some problems this year with Oktoberfest."

Devin interrupted, "Some problems? Ten people were arrested over the weekend. This can't continue, and the town council will discuss how we move forward tonight."

"Ten arrests. Wow, that is not great," Nicole paused. "But do we know how many total visitors we had?"

"I don't have any concrete data, but there has got to be at least a thousand people coming to Marley Creek each weekend day. Nicole, what does Oktoberfest have to do with you? Please tell me no one has been peeing on your lawn," she pleaded, only half joking.

"No, I'm good. It's Zaina that is worried. You see, the thing is…"

Twenty minutes later, Nicole had brought Devin up to speed on the plan to keep Oktoberfest going.

"You know I want the best possible outcome for everyone. We need to make sure our residents are unbothered, and we need to have businesses that are thriving."

"Great, I'll leave it there, and we'll see what happens at the meeting tonight."

Nicole ended the call. She had a couple of hours before she had to leave to walk over to Zaina's, since they had planned to go to the meeting together. She took the time to make a quick dinner and get her stuff ready for the next day. Then she made sure the bed had clean sheets, and that there were some condoms and lubricant in her nightstand.

At six, Nicole walked over to Zaina's shop.

Zaina sat with her head in her hand and listened to Nicole talk about Sean.

"I wish you could see the light in your eyes right now. There is such hope. I can't remember the last time your shoulders weren't a little slumped, your skin a little grey, even your eyes looked dull."

"I'm feeling insulted here, Zaina."

She ignored Nicole and kept talking. "But now, it's like you're alive. Did you change moisturizers? Or is this all the result of some good consistent shagging?"

"Shagging?"

"It's fun to say. I'm also trying to start using brilliant more."

"Okay," Nicole smiled. She was used to her friend's occasional new quirks. "Did you get a subscription to the Acorn channel or something?"

"No, Mike has to go to London in December, and I'm preparing for when he asks me to travel with him."

"Oh! That would be cool." Nicole pursed her lips and squinted her eyes. "Has he ever asked you to go with him on a business trip before?"

"No, but this time is going to be different. He has to be gone for the last two weeks of the year, and we always spend Christmas together, so I'm sure he's going to ask me to go."

"Mm-hmm," Nicole replied noncommittally. She had her doubts when it came to Mike, but as long as Zaina was happy, she wasn't going to put down her boyfriend.

"Enough about me, tell me, how are you feeling about things with Sean? Are you keeping it casual or..." She gave Nicole a long look and leaned forward in her chair.

Nicole's cheeks reddened. "He's coming over after the meeting. Not that it matters, but we haven't been shagging."

"Not yet," Zaina said in a sing-song voice.

"No, not yet," Nicole whispered.

"I'm sorry I'm being a jerk. You can have or not have sex with Sean whenever is best for you. I'm happy if you're happy. Really!"

"Thanks for that," Nicole said and squirmed a little in her seat. "I think tonight is the night, though."

"I knew it! He's the one for you! You're the one for him! Soulmates." Zaina squealed.

Nicole rolled her eyes. "I don't believe in soulmates. It's too mean."

"How can it be too mean?"

"I don't like the idea that there is only one true love for everyone. What if someone gets sick and dies? Then the person left behind is forever alone. It's depressing."

Zaina frowned, "I suppose if you think of it that way it's less romantic. Maybe some people have their one and other people have more than one?"

"I don't need a soulmate. I want a good person who's honest and kind. That's all I need."

Zaina hugged herself. "I love that, and I think you are right. Honesty means that your person respects you, and kindness again means they respect you *and* care for you, above themselves even. From everything I've seen, Sean is that, plus he can cook and he's hot. There, I said it! Your man has those dimples and that thick hair, and let's be honest, he has a great-looking ass. I mean the only bad thing I can say about him is that he isn't broody."

Nicole laughed. "Thanks, I guess?"

"You're the one who scowls in your relationship."

Nicole scowled.

"That's why I'm so happy you're dating Sean! He's good for you and I know you are good for him! I saw the way he looked at you on trivia night. His eyes got all moony, and the way he gave you a few light touches when you both were talking. And later, when he was working, he'd look over at you and smile. It was adorable. He really likes you!"

Nicole's eyes were misty, and she needed to change the subject. "So how have things been going with the business group? Is everyone ready for the meeting?"

"As ready as we can ever be." Zaina looked at her phone. "Speaking of, can you turn the sign to close and lock the door while I shut down the point of sale? We'd better get going!"

Chapter Fourteen

Sean was sitting in front of his laptop at the desk he'd put in the corner of his kitchen. His neck was stiff from spending all day working on a spreadsheet to show the town council the economic impact of Oktoberfest on Marley Creek. Since Sean spent most his waking hours at Jesse's Pub, it hadn't made sense to get a nice desk and chair for his apartment. In fact, it made little sense to him to rent more than a studio apartment when he'd opened a restaurant in Marley Creek.

Even though he'd been here for years now, he'd never put anything on the walls, or even bothered to have a scented candle or a nice diffuser. His décor was devoid of personality and heavy on the beige: beige Berber carpet, beige couch, and tan curtains. Even his comforter was a lighter shade of brown. The only spot of color in his apartment was his unenthusiastic blue betta fish, Hermie.

He contrasted his apartment with the riot of color and textures that made Nicole's home so inviting. He was thrilled to be heading there this evening instead of coming home to his cold, sterile apartment. Now that he was in his third year at the restaurant, and they had steady revenues, maybe it was okay to think about building a life beyond his business.

Sean checked his outfit in the mirror. He was a graphic T-shirt and jeans kind of guy when he wasn't in his chef's whites. Tonight however, he wanted to look like a successful local business person. He was fortunate to be running the restaurant at a profit, given that most restaurants didn't break even in their first few years.

He straightened his tie and pulled on his tweed suit jacket. The well-worn brown jacket had been his grandfather's. It was truly vintage, dating back to just after World War II. Sean had taken care of it over the years he'd owned it, saving it for special occasions or when he needed an extra boost of confidence. The buttons and the elbow patches were actual leather. The tweed itself wasn't nappy. It looked great with his khaki dress pants, and he completed his ensemble with a pair of dark brown dress sneakers. Actual dress shoes were a bridge too far for a man who spent almost all his waking hours in Crocs.

Sean hadn't worn the jacket in a few years and as he looked in the mirror, he realized he looked more like a college professor than the smart business owner vibe he was going for, but then his alarm was going off and he needed to leave. He didn't have the time to change again. He got in his Jeep and headed to Jasper's business. After he pulled up to Hop's Heaven, he texted Jasper to let him know he was waiting for him out front.

"Hey buddy," Jasper said as he opened the car door and folded his six foot three-inch body into the seat. Jasper's hair was tied back, and he was wearing a flannel shirt over one of the Hop's Heaven shirts. He had on jeans and Chelsea boots.

"You look like the first result in Google Images for a craft brewery owner."

"Fantastic because that is exactly the look I was going for tonight." Jasper tapped on his phone's camera and checked his smile.

"You nailed it," Sean said dryly.

Sean backed up and Jasper began messing with his radio, flipping through stations until he found a classic rock station. Then Jasper sat back and tapped on the armrest until they arrived at Marley Creek Town Hall. Sean pulled into the parking lot looking for a space.

"I don't see any spaces. I guess I'll just park on the street." Jasper pointed down the street where a few spots were open about halfway down the block. "Dang," he said under his breath. "The whole town is coming to this meeting."

"That could be a good thing. If they aren't on your side, we can work to get them on your side tonight. If the public is good with Oktoberfest, then that pressures the town council into letting it continue."

"I hope you're right, man." Jasper bit his thumbnail as Sean found a spot and parallel parked. Jasper got out, and Sean reached back to pick up his file filled with data on how Oktoberfest had added to various small businesses' revenues during the five-week period it ran.

Jasper chuckled as he took in Sean's ensemble. "Dude, you look like you're a high school teacher. All you need is some glasses."

"Ha. Ha. I think I look more like a college professor." They raced toward the town hall.

They needed to get their names on the sign-up sheet for public comments, and now it looked like they might have to wait for dozens of other people to talk. Jasper sped ahead of Sean and pulled open the door. The seats in the small meeting room were already filled, and people were standing along the wall.

Sean looked around. There she was. He started grinning like a fool, only he didn't feel like one because he could see her eyes light up when she saw him. She whispered something to her friend with the short, platinum-blonde hair. The woman turned her head, looked at Sean and then Jasper, and her black lipsticked lips turned down. She nodded and pulled out her phone. Sean glanced over at his friend, whose brow had lowered and he'd crossed his arms. Sean didn't need a class in body language to know there was some bad blood between those two.

Nicole sidled next to him, and he put an arm around her, whispering in her ear, "You smell so good, like a jasmine and vanilla cake with lavender frosting. I want to eat you up."

She suppressed a giggle. "Thank you, baby," her voice was husky, and he pulled her closer to him. He wanted to pick her up and carry her out of there and back to his Jeep and ravish her. "It's a body mist Zaina gave me."

"I fucking love it."

She squeezed his hand and took half a step back. "And look at you!" She put her hand on the front of his jacket and smoothed his lapels. "I am loving this..." she slightly pulled on his tie, "ensemble on you. Are you cosplaying as a professor tonight?"

"I don't know. Am I?" He winked at her and ran a hand through his hair.

"The only thing you're missing is glasses."

"Jasper said the same thing."

Nicole laughed, and then sobered, a heat flickering in her eyes. "But seriously, you look even sexier than you do in your chef whites. I love the jacket."

"It was my grandfather's. He gave it to me for my high school graduation. Then he died later that year. It's hard to believe that's been nearly fifteen years now."

Nicole nodded, then she pursed her lips, "Nearly fifteen years? Not practically twenty?"

"What do you mean? I graduated in two thousand and nine."

Nicole's eyes widened, "I guess we never talked about it, but I assumed you were the same age as Jasper and me."

"I've always wanted to date an older woman." Sean elbowed Nicole playfully.

"I've never dated a younger man before." Nicole touched her throat. "I don't know how I feel about this."

"Well, since up until two minutes ago you didn't know and everything was great, I hope you feel fine about it."

Nicole shook her head to clear it and replied, "You're right; it doesn't matter. It's not like you're twenty-two and I'm thirty-six."

"Exactly, we are practically the same age. Except I was finishing up eighth grade when you were graduating high school. Other than that," he shrugged and winked at her.

She stood on her tiptoes and kissed his cheek. "Oh stop! Before I forget, I signed you and Jasper up for the public comments. You speak sixth' and he speaks after you."

"Great," he said, putting his hands in his pockets and rocking on his heels. He wasn't big on public speaking, so he was glad Jasper would be speaking after him. If he floundered, Jasper could clean up the mess.

A grey-haired man wearing a Marley Creek polo gaveled the meeting to order. Nicole quietly made her way back to her seat by Zaina while Sean stood with Jasper at the back of the room. Mayor Devin Belmont began the meeting with the Pledge of Allegiance. Half an hour later, it was time for public comments. Sean was incredibly glad he wasn't the first to talk because he hadn't realized how many incidents had occurred over the past few weeks. Things were not looking good for Jasper right now.

Sean gazed around the room. Zaina was slumped in her chair, Donnie from the bakery was sitting with his hands on his forehead, and Jasper stood with his fists clenched as the first speaker complained about someone recently using her backyard as a urinal. Sean looked to his side to check in on Jasper. His ears were bright red, and his shoulders had drawn forward. Sean nudged him gently with his elbow. "We got this, bro," he whispered.

The second speaker's story was as bad as the first, and it kept going from there. All the speakers before Sean had used their full three minutes to complain about Oktoberfest and ask that it be canceled for the remainder of the season. Butterflies filled his stomach as his name was announced, and he walked up to the podium. He turned and handed a copy of his spreadsheet to each of the council members. Then he stood behind the podium and cleared his throat. He was greeted with a quick burst of feedback that woke up anyone who might have dozed off during the meeting. The noise gave him a start. He jumped as even more adrenaline surged through him. He paused for a moment to gather himself and then began speaking.

"Hi, I'm Sean, the chef and owner of Jesse's Pub. I'm here to ask that the council consider—" His mind went blank; he couldn't remember what he was supposed to say next. The room was so quiet he could hear the two elder councilmen breathing. Sweat began beading on his back, and his collar suddenly felt tight.

He looked up, and there was Nicole, smiling and giving him a thumbs-up. "You got this," she mouthed. And he remembered what came next. "I'm asking that you consider allowing Oktoberfest to continue because it is profitable for the businesses of Marley Creek. If you look at my spreadsheet, you can see the increase in foot traffic and the impact on sales for a wide variety of businesses in the area."

"As many of you know, it's hard to keep a small business going, especially physical locations. We are often just a couple of bad months from closing, so this event helps us to keep the lights on during the lean times we all know show up with the new year." He looked up from his paper, bolstered by the faces nodding in the crowd. "Thank you for your consideration." He turned and nodded to the town council and the mayor, and then made his way on shaky legs back to where he'd been standing.

Jasper walked with casual grace up to the podium. He smiled and nodded at several people in the chairs lining the aisle and then began his public comment. He put his hand on his heart and began speaking, "First and foremost, I'd like to apologize to the town council, our Mayor, and the residents of Marley Creek, especially everyone who was affected by the bad behavior of some of our Oktoberfest guests. I've heard what you had to say, and I've come up with a plan that II believe addresses the issues and would allow this profitable event to continue benefiting Marley Creek. I mean, those sales tax dollars can add up, and those funds could be used for beautification projects to make our Main Street even more inviting for visitors and residents alike."

An alarm went off, ending his three minutes.

Devin turned off the alarm and waved her hand. "Go on, Mr. Kane."

Jasper turned back to the group and resumed his plan, ticking off each bullet point with his hand. "One, as of this afternoon I have increased my liability insurance to ten million dollars. Two, members of our Chamber of Commerce have volunteered to work as additional servers and security. I will donate their pay to the Chamber's scholarship fund. Three, we will close at eleven p.m. instead of one a.m. on Fridays and Saturdays. This should greatly reduce issues that have occurred. Police Chief Henrick, thank you for all your patience. We will do better from here on out, and frankly, I expect not to see you."

The Chief chuckled, and Jasper continued. "I love being part of this wonderful community and to make amends, Hop's Heaven will host a family-friendly autumn event. We'll have pumpkins for decorating, a costume contest for kids and pets, and plenty of food and non-alcoholic drinks."

A few people in the crowd started clapping. Sean, Nicole, Zaina and the other business owners joined in, and soon the entire room was clapping. The little furrow that had developed between Devin's eyebrows smoothed, and Jasper's smile went up to his eyes.

One of the councilmen tapped the gavel. "Order, order, please."

The room quieted down, and Jasper said, "Thank you again for your time. Our first annual Family Fall Fest will be this

Sunday, October sixth, from ten a.m. to four p.m. I look forward to seeing all of you there."

Jasper walked to where he'd been standing at the back of the room with his head held high and his shoulders back.

Sean clapped him on the back. "You did it! Great job!"

Jasper fist-bumped Sean, and then they stood with bated breath as more townspeople spoke. Jasper hung his head a few times as residents spoke of public urination, vomit on the sidewalks, and an amorous couple on a sidewalk bench. Sean didn't want to draw attention to his friend's discomfort, so he didn't say anything. Fortunately, some of those residents were offset by more local business owners talking about how Oktoberfest was important for their businesses, and even the people who were upset seemed mollified by Jasper's solution to the problems.

Finally, it was time for the council to vote on the resolution to close down Oktoberfest. A few minutes later, the final vote was cast, and the resolution failed four to three. Some people groaned, but quite a few people cheered. Jasper made a beeline to talk to residents who had complained during the public comments, and Sean walked over to Nicole and Zaina.

Nicole put her arm around Sean's waist. "You were great, Sean. Your spreadsheet made a difference in the voting."

"I do love data," he said, smiling.

Zaina put up her hand and Sean high-fived her. "We did it!"

"Yes, we did!"

Nicole moved and placed her hand in his. He liked the feeling of her soft hand in his, their fingers entwined. "Are you ready to go?" he asked Nicole.

She nodded, "Yep, but what about Jasper? Did you drive together?"

"We did, but he's good. He said he wanted to walk back no matter the outcome of the vote."

Nicole grinned. "Let's go then."

"I'll see you later, Zaina."

"Have a great night, y'all," Zaina said and winked at them.

Sean and Nicole skirted the small groupings of people scattered around chatting and made their way out of the stuffy room and into the cool fall evening. Leaves were falling from the big oaks and maples that lined the street as they walked along the sidewalk.

"I love this time of year," Nicole gushed, to Sean's surprise. "Why?"

Nicole pursed her lips slightly, then spoke, "I think it's the anticipation, looking forward to the celebrations that are coming soon, the food, gathering with friends and family. The hope for a new and better year." Warmth filled Sean's chest, and he kissed the top of her head. She leaned against his side, and they crossed the street to his Jeep.

Chapter Fifteen

♥

She opened the door, missing the lock twice before she could get the key in. Her hands and whole body were shaking with more excitement than fear, but it was a close call. Sean walked in behind her and then he turned around and closed the door, locking it. He came up behind her as she was hanging up her coat.

Sean whispered in her ear. "Who knew community advocacy could be so hot?"

He moved her hair and kissed the sensitive skin behind her ear. Her skin goose-pimpled, and she shivered as he pulled her back into him. She could feel his arousal, and her heart swelled with pride. Nicole closed the closet door and turned around into his embrace. He bent his head down and began kissing her softly. She kissed back, and as the kiss finished, she lightly tugged on his bottom lip with her teeth. He growled, and she felt the warm vibration of his chest against her. She put her hands under his suit jacket, pushing it off him. "Who knew how hot you'd look in a tweed jacket?" She leaned back from his embrace. "It's giving hot professor. I think that might be my thing."

"Maybe we need to role play?"

"Maybe," she said, undoing his tie and pulling it off. He started to pull out his shirt and she stayed his hands. "No, no, please let me."

Sean stopped and put up his hands. "Feel free to take off all my clothes," he whispered as he lifted an eyebrow.

She pulled out the tails of his shirt and then began unbuttoning it. Finally, she could feel his skin below her palms. His chest was broad and dusted with dark hair. She ran her hands up his chest and stopped to rub his nipples lightly under her thumbs. Then she leaned forward and licked around the hardened left nub and then gave it a little bite.

"You're killing me," Sean groaned.

She pulled Sean over to the couch and pushed him down. He took a moment to unbutton the cuffs of his shirt. Nicole slid onto his lap, her jean-clad legs folded on each side of him. "You're trapped now." She leaned over and started placing kisses down his neck.

He grabbed her ass and said, "Is this alright?" She nodded. He gently started rocking her against him. She savored the friction as he moved her up and down across the zipper that was barely holding his cock back. "I love the way my hands feel on your ass; it's like they were made to grip you like this." His hands dipped down and cradled her. "I want to feel every inch of you. Hell, I can't wait to have my head between your thighs, drinking you in."

Nicole was overwhelmed by the deep tenor of his voice, the smoky musk of his scent, and those words. "Yes, oh yes, I'd like that too." He moved his hands around to her thighs and then moved them up her stomach slowly. As his hands caressed her, she felt her breasts ache with a heaviness and desire she'd barely remembered ever feeling in the past. Her nipples hardened and pressed against her lacy bra. She wanted nothing more than to take off her shirt and bra and have Sean's knife-callused hands on her breasts, gently pulling on her swollen nipples. But she couldn't do it.

She needed the safety of keeping her shirt on. He reached for her shirt, but she pushed his hands off. She took his hand and moved it under her waistband until she could feel his fingers brushing against her clit. Sean froze for a moment, and then he groaned. His eyes filled with lust, and he rubbed her nub with his thumb. Warmth pooled and his thumb slid in her wetness. She jerked as he quickened his pace. Then he was pushing hi lips against hers. Their kiss quickly deepened, and she was tasting him on her tongue. She was soaked through her panties now, and she ground against him.

"Do you want to take this to the bedroom?" Nicole asked him breathlessly.

He gently put her to the side, stood up and held out a hard. "Lead the way."

Nicole loved that about him; he let her make these decisions. She took his hand, and they walked to her bedroom. When they arrived at her door, he gently pushed her against the wall, and he leaned down and gave her a gentle kiss. "We don't have to do anything you don't want to do. If you change your mind at any point, just tell me and we'll stop. I'm in no hurry; I'm not going anywhere. I'm crazy about you," he said as his eyes locked onto hers.

Her skin cooled. She wasn't sure if she could do this. Did she need to tell him more about herself? She kissed him deeply and then pulled back. "Is it a problem if I keep my shirt on?" she blurted.

Sean stopped suddenly, and Nicole's heart dropped; her body filled with icy dread.

"If that's what makes you comfortable, it's fine with me."

"You don't think it's weird?"

"I'm not doing a whole lot of thinking right now." Sean made a trail of kisses on her jaw and pulled Nicole to him. "Right now, the only thoughts in my head are that I really like you and I can't wait to push you down on your bed, lightly of course, and then kiss your neck." His finger touched the side of her neck, trailing down to her collarbone. Sean moved down to her breast and stopped to briefly fondle her nipple through her clothes, and then he traveled down to the waistband of her pants. He tugged and her pants unsnapped. After a second to unzip her pants, he slid his hand inside her panties and cupped her.

"You are so wet." She pulsed with arousal as his fingers moved into her folds.

"I want this so bad," she moaned.

"I can't wait to taste all of you." He pushed two fingers into her and began moving back and forth, and she pressed against him, her mind filled with thoughts of this man. She forced herself to push him from her, and then she took his hand and pulled him into her bedroom. They both pushed off their pants and underwear. Sean was a man of his word, savoring every drop of her juices like she was the best wine he'd ever tasted. He made her come twice before they came together as one, finding their release in the early hours of the morning.

Chapter Sixteen

♥

He slipped out of Nicole's bed, found his clothes and then took a shower. Was that presumptuous of him, to shower in her home? He wasn't usually such an early riser, but he didn't sleep well in other people's beds, even when it was a bed filled with Nicole's luscious curves and the scent of her everywhere. He peeked back into Nicole's room. She was still fast asleep, sprawled across the bed. He was tempted to wake her up, but glancing at the bedside clock, he saw it was only six a.m. and they'd been up late exploring each other. He went to the kitchen to see if he could make coffee and a little breakfast for them.

He was quietly rummaging around in Nicole's cabinet when he realized he didn't have his phone. He walked into the living room and found his jacket on the floor. *Man, what a night,* he thought to himself as he checked his coat pocket and found his phone. The battery was dead. Sean looked around Nicole's living room but didn't see a phone charger anywhere. He went into the kitchen and checked what had to be her junk drawer but no luck there either. He didn't want to wake her up, so he put on his shoes and coat and went out to his Jeep to charge his phone.

He turned the key to accessories and plugged in his dead phone. At the same time, he turned the radio on low and daydreamed as he waited for his phone to get enough juice to start up. His mind's eye replayed her sighs as he'd lapped up her sweet juices. God, she was gorgeous. He checked the clock on the dashboard. Did he have enough time to go back to Nicole's bed? *Ping. Ping. Ping. Ping.* The constant stream of notifications on his phone startled him.

Sean picked up his phone and swiped to unlock it. Stunned, he saw alert after alert from his refrigeration app. When he refurbished the kitchen at Jesse's Pub, he'd splurged on a fancy smart walk-in cooler/freezer with an app. He'd set up the alerts the same day it was installed, and he'd never gotten a notification until three a.m. this morning, and then at four, five, five-fifteen and five-thirty.

ALERT: TEMPERATURE UNSTABLE CODE 14.

ALERT: TEMPERATURE UNSTABLE CODE 15.

ALERT: UNIT NOT RESPONDING.

ALERT: CODE 19.

ALERT: TEMPERATURE ABOVE LIMITS CODE 20.

Sean's heart thumped in his chest. If their cooler/freezer was down, and it looked like it was, then he'd just lost thousands of dollars in frozen goods he needed for this week's menu at Jesse's Pub as well as catering over at Hop's Heaven. In a panic, he started the car and drove over to see what the damage was. He pulled up to the front door of his restaurant and jumped out of his car. When he pulled on the restaurant door trying to open it, he realized he didn't have the key for the door because it was still in the Jeep, which was running. He rushed back, turned it off, and ran to the door. As soon as he opened it, all he could hear was a constant beeping coming from behind the swinging doors. He ran through the dining area and slammed through the swinging kitchen doors. His boots splashed water up his legs, and he skidded to a stop, barely avoiding falling. A small river was streaming out of the cooler toward the drain.

"Argh!" Sean screamed as the beeping continued. The power was clearly on, so it wasn't a power outage. He needed to call the company; he crossed his fingers that the unit was still under warranty. Acid was rising in his throat because he couldn't remember if he'd purchased an extended warranty. Maybe if it wasn't covered, then he could get it repaired or replaced under his business insurance policy. His mind was whirling. Tomorrow was fried chicken night. "Shit!" He spun around, looking at the three cases of whole chickens that were now garbage. Worse than garbage, because all this food waste was going to fill his trash dumpster and he'd have to call for an extra pickup.

He walked out of the cooler, and over to his desk to make calls. First to the waitstaff to let them know Jesse's would be closed tomorrow, and then to the back of the house. He gave the bussers the opportunity to come in and help him clean up, and both of his guys said they'd be able to come in for a few hours. Next, he called the hotline number for his refrigeration unit, and there he got some welcome news. The customer service representative was able to look up Sean's account, and then it turned out he had in fact purchased the extended warranty. A tech would be out by six tonight to evaluate and make repairs. Additionally, the rep told Sean he could contact his insurance agent, and he might be able to put in a claim for all the spoiled food.

Sean made more phone calls, and by ten a.m. he had a pain that started at his eyeballs and made its way to his neck. At first, he thought it was because of the awful hold music he'd been listening to off and on for several hours. Then he realized he hadn't had any coffee, and worse yet, he realized he'd left Nicole's house without saying anything to her! His headache worsened, and a rush of adrenaline and embarrassment flooded him. "Oh, fuck," he said to the piles of slowly rotting food. He picked up his cell phone and hurriedly typed a text.

> SEAN: Nicole, no excuse, but I had an emergency at the restaurant. Sorry I left without waking you up. I will make it up to you. Call me tonight.

As he was trying to decide if he should end the text with a kissy face or winky face emoji plus a peach emoji, his phone rang. It was Jasper calling. He'd been waiting frantically for Jasper's call back. He exited the text screen and took Jasper's call. Sean needed to see if he could move a food delivery for today to the rail car so he wouldn't have to cancel on the farmer.

Chapter Seventeen

Nicole's alarm started chiming at six thirty-five a.m., and she rolled over to hit the snooze. She was utterly exhausted, and it took her brain a moment to catch up and remind her of the night before. It hit her with full force, and she rolled over away from her phone hoping to find the six foot plus inches of Sean taking up all the space next to her. She'd love a good morning cuddle. Her bed was empty though, so she got up, went over to her dresser, got out a pair of pajama bottoms and pulled them on.

She walked down the hall, hoping to find Sean in her kitchen. She walked slowly as she didn't hear anyone stirring, and she wondered if maybe he had left her bed and gone to sleep on the couch. Nicole was sure he must be around her house somewhere because he wasn't the kind of guy who'd just leave. From her living room, she could see that her driveway was empty. So, he had left. She let out a heavy sigh. She thought Sean was different, but it looked like he'd left her, just like Duncan did. Men were the worst. *Wait, maybe he left to go get coffee and donuts for them to share? Was that a possibility?* She twisted a lock of her hair. She'd seen that happen in at least three or four Hallmark movies.

She looked out the window and down the street just in case he might be on his way back, and this was just a silly misunderstanding on her part that they'd laugh about later. Then she remembered her life wasn't a Hallmark movie. She closed the blinds and went to get ready for work.

There had been plenty of days in the past when she'd gone to work even though she wasn't feeling her best because she needed the distraction. Those days had dragged because she was in pain or so tired from radiation she could barely keep her eyes open. Then there was today. Today felt like a year. She kept thinking back to the night before and second guessing, trying to figure out why Sean had left. What sign did she miss? Was it the shirt thing? He'd clearly enjoyed himself, but maybe he panicked. Repeatedly, Nicole stared blankly into nothing. She'd been so distracted by Sean ghosting her she'd missed the first fifteen minutes of her lunch and then when she got back from lunch she intercommed the wrong classroom three times before she'd gotten it right.

She'd also started and deleted at least twenty texts to Sean and about that many to the group chat. Fortunately, she'd stopped herself. Right now, her plan was to go home and hide under her covers until it was time to go to work tomorrow. In fact, she thought this was a solid plan for the foreseeable future. Maybe at some point Sean would text her, or she'd have a couple of drinks and text him.

She dropped her purse and jacket on her coffee table, toed off her shoes and made herself a tomato and grilled cheese sandwich. As she ate her early dinner, she stared at her phone.

She could just delete Sean's contact. That was one way to make sure she never drunk-dialed him. Maybe she'd do that tomorrow. For now, she was going to take a nice hot bath, then take a Benadryl and go to bed. Tomorrow was another day.

Chapter Eighteen

Sean was a guy who needed a good seven hours of sleep to function. Being on his feet for at least ten hours a day most days of the week, while handling knives, boiling water, and cranky customers, he required rest to make sure he didn't screw something up.

Unfortunately, he'd barely gotten any sleep for several days now. On Tuesday, it was because of a fantastic night with Nicole. Wednesday, he'd been at Jesse's Pub until after two a.m. disposing of all the wasted food and cleaning. Then on Thursday, he'd had to beg suppliers most of the day to get orders in, and that was another day of being closed. They were finally back open on Friday, but he'd tossed and turned all night because Nicole had ghosted him.

He'd spent yesterday back and forth between Jesse's and Hop's Heaven at least five times getting everything ready for the Fall Family Fest. As if that wasn't enough, he'd been interviewing sous chefs to take Charlie's place all week. The upside to that was he'd found Lucas, who'd be starting this week. Lucas was only twenty-five, but he'd grown up in the restaurant business, and Sean had high hopes he'd be a great fit for Jesse's Pub.

He was glad that Jasper was too busy to ask him about the bags under his eyes or Nicole. Sean didn't know what to make of Nicole. They'd had such a great night together. Could she still be mad that he'd left and hadn't contacted her for a few hours? Man, the last thing he'd wanted to do was leave her bed and go deal with soggy French fries and rotting fryers. He shuddered at the thought of that massive pile of wasted chickens. He thought she would be understanding. She knew how important Jesse's Pub was to him. His livelihood was the restaurant, and it had been an emergency. Sean didn't do drama.

Maybe this was a red flag. His shoulders slumped. He knew it was nuts, but he'd been making plans with Nicole in mind, and now all that was for nothing? At times like these, it was hard to cling to his positive attitude, but he was going to do his best.

Yesterday it had rained like crazy, but today the sun was out, and Jasper had gotten a ton of hay put down so all the kids and their parents wouldn't be walking around in a muddy mess. Not only were Sean's refrigeration problems behind him, but he'd gotten a great deal on all-natural hot dogs for the fest today. He'd offered to donate the food for the event because he knew that pulling this off was crucial for him as well as Jasper. But Jasper had refused to accept that deal, so Sean was glad he'd be able to get the best food possible at the lowest cost for Jasper. He was feeling better already. The focus today needed to be on Marley Creek residents enjoying the fest. He was going to make sure that happened, even if he had to dress up and entertain the kids himself while their parents enjoyed a beer and a brat.

Chapter Nineteen

Zaina knocked on Nicole's door. Nicole had managed to avoid most of Zaina's texts and having to rehash the Sean incident up until now. Today, however, was the fest at Hop's Heaven, and there was no way Nicole could get out of this. She'd rather avoid talking about Sean or seeing him, but it was probably better to just go with the flow today. If she bailed, Zaina would kill her.

Nicole's plan was to keep the focus on Zaina and avoid talking about Sean. She poured herself and Zaina a cup of coffee.

"We have some time before we have to leave for Hop's Heaven. Would you like a piece of apple cake with your coffee?"

"That sounds great. I had to run some errands this morning and then I had to get everything ready for my booth, so I didn't have time to eat."

"How have things been going with Oktoberfest?"

"Nic, so far so good. We had the Marley Creek Business Association meeting the other day, and Chief Hendrick shared with us that complaints have completely fallen off! We did it!"

"That's awesome! I'm so glad it's working out." Nicole paused, unsure if she should ask about Jasper, but her curiosity won out. "You helped on Thursday, right? How's it going with Jasper there? I know you aren't a fan."

Zaina, "Oh, he doesn't bother me at all," she said, her voice rising an octave.

"Mm-hmm," Nicole said again.

"Besides, I barely saw him when I was there. I helped with the trivia night people, and he was at the main bar and in the actual brewery. Not that it would matter."

"I see."

"Stop! Let's go over what's happening today. I'm going to have a little booth there and dress up like a fortune teller to do tarot card readings for the Marley Creek Kids Christmas Fund."

"You'll be great. You're super good at being very dramatic."

"Is that a compliment or…?"

"I'm just kidding! What I mean is, you're good at acting. I still remember you in all the plays and musicals in high school. You should do that now."

"What do you mean?"

"Community theater! You know you could be in one of the productions Oak Community College does. You don't have to take a class, just live in the college district."

"I don't know about that. I'm busy with the store and spending time with Mike."

"Speaking of Mike, where is he today? Is he going to be at the fest?" Nicole knew she was treading on thin ice here. The mess that had happened with Sean really didn't give her any credibility to poke at Zaina's relationship with Mike. Still, she couldn't help asking even though she knew Mike wouldn't be at the fest, because Mike didn't show up for Zaina. He only came around when he needed something from her.

Zaina pursed her lips and put her fork down. "He really wanted to come, but he had a work emergency."

"What does he do again?"

"Nic, you don't remember? He's in insurance. He works with actuaries."

"Oh yes, that's it. I don't know why I forget. Huh, I wonder what the emergency was."

"It was one of those things where someone else was supposed to complete a presentation for a client and they didn't get it done, so Mike had to step in and save the day."

"He's a real trooper." Nicole said dryly.

Zaina smiled broadly. "He's working really hard to make sure he gets a promotion soon. He has been talking about how this promotion would mean a serious increase in salary, plus he'd have stock options. Once he has that financial security, you know what that means?"

"Time to settle down?" Nicole knew what Zaina wanted to hear. This was a call and response they went through every couple of months when Zaina started getting anxious about where things were headed with Mike.

"That's it exactly," Zaina said, picking up her fork and taking a big bite of cake. She chewed slowly. "This is so good. Did you make it?"

"It's from work; Nancy brought it in. It's delicious, isn't it?"

"So good," Zaina nodded and spoke with her mouth full.

"Back to Mike. I know you don't like the tarot cards, but every time I do a reading focused on me and Mike, the cards tell me something big is happening in December. That's when he is going to London for work. So obviously, I'm going with! And while we are there, I just know he is going to pop the question!"

Zaina hopped a little in excitement.

Nicole chose her words carefully. "I would love that for you!" and then she changed the subject.

"How's everything looking for the fest today?"

"Everything's coming together nicely. I think my fortune teller booth will be a hit since we are in spooky season. Donnie from Books and Breads made a ton of pumpkin cookies and is supplying frosting and sprinkles so all the kids can decorate cookies. Jasper is providing everyone with a pumpkin, and then we have a ton of other business association members that are running the costume contest for adults and kids. Plus, everyone donated prizes. I'm so glad we are going to pull this off."

"Don't jinx it!"

"Good point," Zaina laughed. "We are a superstitious bunch. I don't know what I was thinking!"

Zaina looked at the clock on the stove. "We'd better get going." Then she added, "Don't think I didn't notice how you got me talking and fed me food to distract me from giving you the third-degree about Sean."

Nicole's face drooped. She'd tried. "Busted," she said, her face bright red.

On the way to the fest, Nicole began telling Zaina about Sean. They arrived at Hop's Heaven and unloaded Zaina's car, taking her supplies over to a canopy that had a table underneath. Nicole followed Zaina's directions and soon her booth was set up.

"So, he didn't call?"

"Nope."

"Are you sure there wasn't like a note?"

"I looked all over. I even moved the furniture in the living room, nothing."

"And he didn't text you?"

Nicole unlocked her phone and showed it to Zaina. "See? No texts."

"Wow, based on what I saw of you two at the Town Council meeting, that makes no sense. Plus, when I did Sean's cards, well, this is not in his character. Could there be some sort of miscommunication?"

"I don't see how, but anything is possible, I suppose," Nicole shrugged.

"Nicole, you know I am always on your side. Team Nicole forever."

Nicole nodded vigorously.

"So whatever happens, I'll follow your lead, but I have to say, I would not be surprised if there was an important reason why he left and maybe some miscommunication is going on. Mercury is in retrograde right now."

Nicole slumped down in her chair. "I feel so stupid. Either I totally misread the situation and he's a jerk, or something happened, and I should have reached out to him by now. It's a mess. I hate this kind of thing. I just want to go home and crawl back into bed."

Zaina got up and stood in front of her friend. She held out her hands, and Nicole took them. She pulled Nicole up to her feet. "What we are not going to do is wallow our lives away. Let's go find Jasper and see where you are working today."

"Alright, let's go. I know I better listen to you if you are willing to talk to Jasper."

"The things I do for my friends." Zaina grumbled with a smile, then went into the brewery to see the schedule for the fest.

"Well, that worked out well for me," Zaina said as they walked back outside.

Nicole crossed her arms. "It sure did. You didn't have to talk to Jasper, but for me not so much."

Zaina laughed, "Look at it this way, you'll soon have all your questions answered and you can go from there."

"No chance I can go home right now? Call off sick?"

"No, ma'am." Zaina pulled her friend by the hand over to the rail car where Nicole was scheduled to work with Sean for the duration of the fest.

Chapter Twenty

♥

Just before the fest was scheduled to begin, Sean realized he'd left the containers of mustard and grilled onions back at Jesse's Pub. Could they have brats or hot dogs without mustard or grilled onions? He supposed so, but how would that reflect on Jesse's Pub? He checked his watch. If he left now, he could be back with the items soon after the fest started. He thought it was safe to assume there wouldn't be a line for brats and dogs right out of the gate. He let one of the volunteers know he'd be back in fifteen minutes and hustled back to Jesse's Pub.

By the time he returned with the toppings, the parking lot was full, and Sean had to drive to the overflow lot to park. Speed walking back to the brewery, he felt more and more flustered. He prided himself on being ready to go for every event he catered, and now he wasn't at his station as the fest began. Sean hadn't realized how many Marley Creek residents would show up at the start of the fest. He'd figured people would start coming in full force around noon.

The weather had cooled enough that he was wearing a light flannel jacket over the neon orange First Annual Family Fest T-shirt Jasper had made for the day. Now sweat was trickling down his back as he weaved through families with strollers, couples with dogs on leashes, and volunteers arriving to help. He had to admit, he'd thought neon orange was a terrible color choice for the T-shirts when Jasper gave him his, but it made it very easy to locate a volunteer amongst the crowd.

Finally, he was almost back to his rail car, and not a moment too soon, as a couple of people were already standing in front waiting for food. He rushed through the door, his face ruddy, and set down the heavy tubs.

"What can I get you?" he asked as he turned, and there was that smile. "Hey, ah, there, I thought ah..." His shock at seeing Nicole had frozen his tongue. *You big dummy, of course she's here*. Now maybe he'd find out why she didn't bother to return his text.

Nicole's cheeks were so red that they almost matched her lush lips. His heart started pounding. Gosh, he'd missed her. He wanted to give her a hug, at a minimum, but he clenched his fists. He had no clue where he stood with her.

Nicole pointed at her shirt and said, "I'm here to help you." Sean noticed she scowled as she spoke. Guess she was mad at him. Even though she was giving him an evil eye, he couldn't help but notice how cute she looked with her glossy lips turned slightly down. And the way she was fuming made the rise and fall of her chest push up her breasts in a way he found difficult to pull his eyes from.

"Ahem," Zaina cleared her throat, and Sean startled; he'd forgotten anyone else was there.

Zaina waved her arms in their flowy black and red sleeves and said, "I'll leave you two to whatever this is. Y'all play nice." She made a 'keeping my eyes on you' gesture to them and then flounced off toward her fortune teller tent where there was already a line of teenage girls waiting.

Sean thought it would be best to start with business. "Come back here and let me show you what we are doing today." He held the door open, and she walked around and into the railcar. That scent of hers hit him as soon as she was through the door. Before he could stop himself, Sean reached out to touch her arm, but just before making contact, he pulled back. He didn't know what she wanted, and he didn't have any rights to her. He balled his hands into fists.

"I've got everything set up. We have brats for the adults, hot dogs for the kids, and they can pick a bag of chips and or an apple. We are only doing food and bottled water. For all the other drinks, they need to go into the main building. Sound good?"

Nicole avoided eye contact; she looked down at the food on display instead of at him. He wanted to put his finger under her chin and tilt her head up so she would look into his eyes. Just the mere presence of her in his space was making his nerves tingle.

"Makes sense," Nicole said flatly and walked over to a box of latex gloves. She pulled on the gloves and turned to look out at the festivities.

"Listen," Sean began, "I'm sorry I left the other day. If it hadn't been an emergency, I would have been there, but I think you should've cut me some slack. You could've replied to my text at least." His jaw clenched in annoyance.

"What are you talking about? You didn't text me."

Sean stared at Nicole, mouth agape. "Of course I did! You think I would just leave and not say anything? After that night? Like it was nothing?"

Nicole cleared her throat and gestured with her head; a family was heading right toward them.

"Hey friends, what can I get for you?" Sean greeted them. One brat with onions and three hot dogs plain. A few minutes later, Sean and Nicole were alone again.

"I didn't know what to think," Nicole said, her teeth gritted. "And I'm telling you, I didn't get a text."

"I sent one! How could you not have gotten it?" He said, his voice rising in frustration.

Nicole pushed out a breath and ran a hand through her hair. "I don't know! All I know is I didn't get it and I still don't understand why you just left! Of course, I didn't call you! Put yourself in my shoes. If we'd been at your place and I just left, and didn't leave a note, or call or text, what would you have done?"

Sean paused for a moment thinking, and another family came up to get food. Nicole served them, and Sean opened a new package of buns. "I would have sent you a quick text and asked if everything was okay. That's what I would have done."

Nicole frowned and hugged herself. "I guess that's just not the way I work. When I didn't hear from you at all on Wednesday, I figured you ghosted me or you were dead in a ditch."

Sean put his hands out in surrender. "I'm sorry, I really did text you."

Nicole took out her phone, unlocked it, and pulled up her text. She clicked on Sean. "See, nothing since before the council meeting."

Sean's face fell and his shoulders dropped. "I'm so sorry. I wonder what happened? Let me check my phone." Sean took off his gloves and swiped through his phone, and pulled up Nicole. And then he saw it. The message he thought he'd sent was still there. He'd never hit the send arrow.

"Well, shit. It's all my fault."

"What happened?"

Sean showed Nicole his phone. As she read, her icy demeanor melted away. She grimaced and covered her face with her hands. "I'm so sorry. I had you all wrong."

Sean walked closer to her. "Can I give you a hug?" Nicole nodded, her eyes glossy, and Sean wrapped her in his arms. He nuzzled the crown of her head with his chin. "It's my fault too. I got so wrapped up in the mess happening at Jesse's, I didn't check to make sure the text was sent, and I didn't bother to call you."

"Can you forgive me?" Nicole asked, a plaintive note in her tone.

Sean felt a sharp pain in his chest. She looked so sad. He rubbed at his own chest and said, "Of course I can. All I ask is that instead of assuming the worst-case scenario if you don't hear from me, that you talk to me. And I'll do the same for you." He noticed she had goosebumps along her forearms, so he rubbed them as he continued. "I'm quite fond of you, darling. Let's not mess up a good thing." Her eyes shining, she stood on her tiptoes and gave him a kiss.

"Mommy, can I get a hot dog?" a voice said, and they turned to see another family ready for food. One family led to a group of teens and then an older couple, and soon there was a line twenty people deep, and they were in the weeds working quickly to feed all the hungry fest goers.

Chapter Twenty-One

♥

Nicole was wrung out, and her feet were sore from standing. She was glad that she'd worn her most comfortable sneakers for the day. She checked her watch. Only half an hour to go.

"Think we'll make it?" she asked Sean.

"The onions are gone. We have two brats and," he paused and checked the slow cooker, "six hot dogs left." Then he turned and looked at the fest which was still filled with people talking, laughing, and kids running around.

Sean shook his head. "If I were a betting man, I'd say we are going to run out of brats and dogs, but we should be okay on chips and apples." Nicole leaned on the counter, rested her head on her hand, and watched the crowd.

Sean leaned next to Nicole and copied her stance. "Penny for your thoughts?"

"I noticed that quite a few of the kids from school are here and it's fun to see them in the wild, so to speak."

Sean chuckled and nudged her with his shoulder. "In the wild, that's about right. Look," he gestured with his head, "that little Barbie is literally stomping her feet and screaming."

"Her mom looks like she's had quite enough," Nicole said. "Looks like it's time for Barbie to go back in the box."

"Yikes," Sean said, and they watched Barbie push her mom away. "Do you recognize that kiddo?"

Nicole gave the little girl a long look. "No, she doesn't look familiar."

"She kind of looks like your friend, Zaina."

Nicole peered at the girl, "Well, she's got the sassy attitude down. Poor thing is probably overstimulated."

Sean nodded, then his face softened. "Aww, it's a little lion. What a cutie."

Nicole looked over to see a dad dressed all in silver with an oil funnel on his head. In his arms was a toddler boy wearing a fuzzy lion costume. The boy's chubby-cheeked little face peeked out of the mane. He was laughing, and the dad gave him a kiss on the cheek and then set him in a wagon. There was another boy in the wagon who looked to be about five years old and was wearing a scarecrow costume.

"Looks like they have a Wizard of Oz family costume. The mom must be around here somewhere as Dorothy. I do love group costumes."

Nicole let out an awkward bark of laughter. She didn't love group costumes, and she wondered if his moony eyes were related to love for the Halloween season or if he was yearning to have children.

"Do you ever think about having kids?" Sean casually asked.

Nicole stiffened and stood up warily. "I can't have kids," she blurted, a blush quickly creeping up her neck. Sean froze suddenly, and Nicole's heart dropped. Her stomach roiled, and a sour taste filled her mouth.

"Okay. That's good to know—" he continued speaking, but static filled Nicole's ears. She could not do this. She turned to leave the rail car when Zaina burst in the door.

"Nic, Devin needs our help now!"

"I gotta go," she said to Sean, and ran out the door after Zaina, grateful she had the excuse to walk away from Sean. Devastated by the sudden thought that they weren't going to make it, Nicole felt tears well behind her eyes. Once again, her broken body was coming between her and happiness. Zania grabbed her hand and pulled her along. "What's going on?" Nicole asked.

Zaina picked up her long, flowy skirt so that she could walk quickly toward the brewery without tripping. Nicole double-stepped to keep pace with Zaina. "Devin arranged for her babysitter to help watch the boys at the fest, but she canceled, so Devin came by herself with the twins today."

"Oh no, she didn't."

"Yep, she didn't want to miss the fest, her being the mayor and all. She wanted to make an appearance, and it's not like you can come to the First Annual Family Fest and not bring your kids, right?"

"True, but these are the twins."

"Also, true."

"Anyway, while Devin was schmoozing some constituents and taking some credit for how well the fest was going, the twins took off and went into the brewery."

"And what's the big deal?"

"They went into the brewery part of the brewery!"

"Oh!" The lightbulb went off in Nicole's head. The twins were not in the bar part of the brewery. Somehow, they'd managed to get into the back where the beer was brewed. "This is bad. Good Lord, how did that happen?"

"It's the twins. The question should almost be 'How could it not happen!'"

Zaina led Nicole around to a plain metal door at the back of the building. She knocked twice, and Devin opened the door.

"Thank God you're here, Nic," Devin said, throwing her arms around Nicole.

"Where's Jasper?" Nicole asked.

"We aren't sure. I'm hoping the three of us can get the twins out of here without anyone having to call the fire department."

"Are they okay?" Nicole said loudly.

Devin crossed her arms. "They are perfectly fine. They are just refusing to get out of there and I can't pull them out." She pointed.

Nicole's mouth dropped open. The boys were on the other side of the large metal grate that separated the fermenters from the rest of the brewery floor. The grate was about five feet high and had slats that were about five inches apart. "How did this happen?"

"I suppose the same way they got out of their cribs and made it out to the garage when they were two. Give them five minutes unsupervised and they will amaze you."

"You really need a nanny, Dev," said Zaina.

"You don't say, Captain Obvious."

"Sorry, I know I'm not helping, but I did run and get Nicole."

"True, and I'm not sure exactly how I can help…" Nicole pondered.

"Nicole, you've worked at a school for fifteen years. You know how to speak these kids' language," Devin said.

"You know I just work in the office; I'm not a teacher or a social worker."

"Don't sell yourself short, Nic. You're better with kids than I am," Devin proclaimed.

Nicole laughed. "You're their mom!"

"I'm pretty sure that's most of the problem," Zaina said.

"Zaina!" Nicole exclaimed.

"No, I'm with her on this one. I think I'm the last person these two scamps will listen to," Devin grumbled. "Honestly, Nic, you're my best friend. I just need you here." Her eyes pleaded with Nicole.

"Of cour—"

"Hey, Nic!" yelled Devin's son, Liam.

"Hey, buddy." Nicole said, "Whatcha doing back there?"

"Lost my hat."

"You lost your hat?"

"Fwanklin rew it.

"Franklin threw your hat?"

Liam nodded furiously. Franklin was wedged under one of the fermenters with his head down and his arms wrapped around his knees.

Nicole looked at Devin and Zaina, "Do you two see a hat anywhere?" They both pointed up. On top of one of the stainless steel, ten-foot-tall fermenters lay a blue baseball hat.

Nicole said, "Well, I guess that explains what happened. Jeez, Franklin can really throw."

"Once we get out of this mess and I tell Ben what happened, he'll sign both of them up for T-ball for sure," Devin said wryly.

Zaina gathered her dress and pulled it off, leaving her in a black shirt and black yoga pants. She handed the voluminous dress to Nicole. "Here, hold on to this. Maybe I can fit through the slats in this gate."

Nicole took the dress, and Zaina attempted to wedge herself between the slats. She was able to get halfway through the space in between, but no matter which way she tried, her head was just a little too big.

Devin looked ready to pull out her hair, "Girl, your head's too big."

"Dammit!" Zaina shouted and pulled herself out from between the two slats.

Nicole looked at the bottom of the grate. There were a few inches between it and the floor.

"Zaina, what if you tried to squeeze under the grate? I would do it myself, but there isn't any way my butt is going to fit under it."

Zaina rolled her eyes. "Is now really the time to remind me you have a great ass and mine is flat?"

Nicole flashed a smile. "Sorry."

Devin stood holding the bars on the gate as if was willing herself to become She Hulk so she could pull the bars apart and retrieve her children via brute strength.

"Do you think you can fit?" She asked, her voice rising an octave.

Nicole handed Zaina her windbreaker. "Here, put this on so you don't get scraped by the metal."

Zaina zipped up the jacket and then walked over to the gate. "I think I should try going feet first, then you can push me?"

Nicole shrugged. "It's worth a shot."

Devin remained at the gate, her knuckles white as she held on. Zaina tucked the jacket into her pants, then got down on her stomach and began scooching back under the gate. Nicole kneeled down and put her hands on Zaina's shoulders and began pushing. Things were going great until she tried to get her thighs through.

"Looks like your runner's thighs have done us in." Devin said.

"I haven't run in ages." Zaina huffed. "Mike hates it."

"We can talk about that later. What are we going to do now? I need my babies."

Nicole sat on the ground and looked over at Franklin under the tank. "I hate to say this, I really do, but Devin, do you think Franklin is stuck under the tank? Do you think he can move?" Devin's face blanched.

"Liam, baby, come over here."

"No Mama, I can't leave Fwanklin."

"You are such a good brother," Devin began and Liam burst out in tears.

"He-he stuck, and it's m-m-me fault."

"Oh baby, it's okay. Franklin knows you love him, right, Franklin?"

Franklin didn't say anything. Devin froze and her eyes went wide. "Is he unconscious?" she squeaked.

Nicole and Zaina spun first to look at Franklin and second to hold Devin up as her knees buckled.

"Franklin, honey, say something to your Mama," Nicole pleaded.

"Mama Sta-wuck!"

Devin sagged in relief, and Nicole held her up. "Devin," said Nicole, "you have to trust me." She held Devin's hands and looked in her eyes. "We are going to push Zaina up and over and she is going to get the boys. We got this, and if anything else happens, we are going to give up and call for help. Okay? Either way, it's going to be okay. Look at me. Why are those shoulders around your ears? Shake them out and take a deep breath."

Devin shook her shoulders and arms, then took a deep breath.

Nicole got down on her hands and knees. "Z, climb on my back."

"Are you sure you want to do this, Nicole?" Zaina asked.

"I'm sturdier than I look. Devin, get ready to boost Zaina over once she's on my back."

Zaina gave her friend a hug. "It's going to be okay. We'll get Franklin unstuck."

Devin rubbed her hands together. "Let's do this!"

Zaina stepped onto Nicole's back. Nicole couldn't help but let out a grunt. "I'm sorry, Nicole!" Zaina said, and then she reached up and put her hands on the top of the grate. Then Devin began pushing her up and Zaina was able to pull herself up enough to get her knee on the top, then her other foot, and then she was over and landing on the floor with a thud.

"Are you okay?" asked Nicole and Devin in unison.

Zaina got to her feet and brushed herself off. "I'll be fine."

Nicole and Devin stood at the gate like teens waiting to get in to see their favorite rock band. Only this was more serious. Liam ran over and threw his arms around Zaina's legs. She took his hand and said, "Liam, let's go get Franklin unstuck."

"Yay!" said Liam, and he skipped back over to where Franklin was. He got down on the floor and put his face close to his brother's. "You be okay now, Fwanklin."

"I wanna go home," Franklin cried.

"You okay," comforted Liam.

Devin was quietly crying while Nicole rubbed her back. "It's almost over. They are going to be fine."

"Franklin, does anything hurt?" Zaina asked.

"Nu-uh." He shook his head.

Zaina smiled, "Let's get you out of there." He was stuck on his side. It wasn't clear how he was stuck, so Zaina ran her hand up his leg and then around to his back. She could feel that his shirt was stuck on the bottom of the tank. "Franklin, don't be scared. I'm going to pull hard on your shirt."

Franklin nodded his head, staring at her with his big brown eyes while Liam looked on, his eyes wide. "One, two, pull!" She tugged as hard as she could, and a loud rip filled the air. Franklin wiggled out from under the tank and got up, a big hunk of his shirt now missing. Zaina leaned back, hand to her chest and looked up, "Thank the goddess. He's fine."

On the other side of the metal gate, Nicole and Devin were locked in a hug, swaying back and forth. Zaina got to her feet. Nicole and Devin separated, and then in the blink of an eye Franklin and Liam had run to the gate, dropped to the ground, and squirmed their way underneath and right into their mother's arms. Everyone was crying; from behind a deep voice shouted, "What in the world is going on?"

Zaina gave Jasper a weak wave, while Devin began using all her lawyerly skills to explain the situation.

A short time later, Jasper had calmed down enough that he unlocked the gate, letting Zaina out. He'd even gotten a ladder and climbed up to retrieve Liam's hat. Zaina gave quick hugs to Nicole and Devin and made a beeline for the door, avoiding Jasper. Jasper kicked Devin, Nicole and the kids out of the brewery, mumbling something about getting an alarm for the back door. Outside, Nicole found Devin's wagon, helped get the boys situated, and then they walked to Devin's car. Devin had insisted that Zaina and Nicole come over for a celebration for saving her kids.

"I know it's been a super scary day for you. Do you want me to spend the night? I haven't gotten to help tuck in the boys in ages," Nicole offered.

The furrow between Devin's perfectly plucked eyebrows softened, "Would you?"

"Of course," Nicole said, and they left the fest.

Chapter Twenty-Two

♥

Sean dumped the hot dog water in the railcar sink. One lone hot dog had been left floating in the oily water at the end of the fest, and if that wasn't a metaphor for his day, he didn't know what was. After Nicole had taken off, he'd had a few stragglers looking for food, and then it was time to clean up. He was torn between taking his time in hopes that Nicole was planning to come back and say goodbye to him and the urgency he had to get back to Jesse's Pub where an engagement party was due to arrive in two hours and twenty minutes. Thank goodness his refrigeration system was back in working condition. That had allowed him to do all his prep for the party yesterday.

Once everything was loaded up in his foldable wagon, Sean pulled down the overhead shutters and mopped his way to the door. He locked it behind him and sent a quick text to Nicole.

SEAN: I'm heading out. Are you still here?

Sean spent a couple of minutes double-checking the wagon, making sure he had his keys and took a quick look through his texts on his phone, just in case she was still there and was walking over. When she didn't respond, he started the long walk to his car.

As he walked by the main brewery building, he looked for Nicole in the sea of orange volunteer shirts but didn't see her. He didn't know what the emergency was that Zaina had dragged Nicole off to. Unable to help himself, he pouted a little wishing he didn't have to rush off to work at a private party. He'd like to know what was going on with Nicole's friend, Devin. By the looks of things at the brewery, whatever the emergency was, it had been resolved. He daydreamed how nice it would be to kick back with a pint of Jasper's award-winning Oktoberfest beer in one hand and his other arm around Nicole. But off to work he must go.

Once he got to his car, he checked his phone again to see if Nicole had texted him back, but she hadn't. Sean sighed and put on one of his favorite upbeat playlists to get in the mood for work. He'd had a little pity party, and now it was time to get his game face on. It was a lucky thing to have this event so soon after the cooler meltdown. He'd lost a few grand and several of his employees had lost shifts they couldn't afford to lose because of the refrigeration malfunction. Now they had a chance to make up some of that ground.

Before he knew it, two hours had passed, and the partygoers had arrived. He'd forgotten that this was an engagement between two high school sweethearts who had reunited at their fiftieth high school reunion here in town last year. Sean really got a kick out of seeing the happy couple hand in hand as they walked around thanking their guests.

Sean noticed that on a few occasions when they weren't together the future groom would watch his bride-to-be with a smile on his face and sparkling eyes. Sean felt heat radiating through his chest as he imagined what it would be like if it were his engagement party. How he would follow Nicole with his eyes, watching as she savored their dinner and as she spoke excitedly with Zaina and Devin.

What a time Nicole would have trying to decide who would be her maid of honor. And on his part, if he invited all his half-and step-siblings, would they even have room at Jesse's Pub for everyone? Did he need to invite his various stepmothers and stepfathers as well? His mood soured a little. He shook himself to end his daydream and went back into the kitchen to start plating the desserts.

After the engagement party was over and the restaurant was cleaned up, he finally made his way home. Sean let himself into his apartment and slid out of his Crocs. He yawned so wide his jaw popped. He shuffled to his bedroom and pulled pajama bottoms out of his dresser drawer. Then, he brushed his teeth and turned on the shower. He tried to lather up and shower, but the warmth of the water only made him that much more tired. The long day, the joy of spending time with Nicole, coupled with not getting to finish their conversation, had spent him. He toweled off, threw on his pajamas, and fell into bed.

***

Nicole woke Monday morning, and for a few seconds, she'd forgotten all about Sean. Then it came back to her. She checked her phone and saw his message from last night. It still sat at the top of her texts unread. She clicked the text, read it, but didn't reply. What would be the point of replying? Even if he said he didn't care that she couldn't have kids, he was a young guy, and he probably didn't even realize he'd want kids of his own. What she was doing was for the best in the long run.

She wasn't what he'd need when his biological clock started ticking. And at this point she didn't have the emotional bandwidth to deal with a long conversation about her inadequacies as a woman. Nicole had done enough of that when Duncan had left, and since then, she'd spent far too much time focusing on what she didn't have to offer. She just wanted to go back to her calm, structured days. Work, home, time with friends, and the occasional trip to see her parents. She needed to keep her peace intact. She kept telling herself it was a liberation to be free of Sean and any expectations for the future. Maybe she'd run into him at the school years from now when he had a child of his own. It was almost to where she could honestly wish nothing but the best for him, at least that's what she was telling herself.

From the moment she walked into work, she was greeted with a parade of problems. First, three teachers were out with the flu, and each of them had a brand new sub filling in. Mr. Steve, the janitor, slipped while cleaning up a hallway water spill, and they had to call the ambulance. Then there was a drop-in safety inspection from the state. Nicole hadn't had a moment to think about Sean or even to sit down all day. Finally, at two o'clock, order was restored.

Nancy walked back into the office. "I will be so glad when Principal Adams is back from that conference. Who schedules a week-long conference for elementary principals in the fall? Isn't that what summer is for?"

"It's completely ridiculous!" Nicole agreed, half paying attention. Now that things had quieted down, she had time to think about Sean. She clenched her fists and tried to banish his handsome face from her mind. She loved the way he laughed at his own bad jokes, and when he did, it made his eyes crinkle and his dimples pop out in the midst of the scruff that covered his perfect chin and strong jawline. Warmth pooled low in her abdomen. This was going to be harder than she thought.

"Nicole, Nicole," Nancy snapped her fingers in her face, trying to get her attention.

Nicole shook her head, coming out of her daydream. "I'm sorry. What were you saying, Nancy?"

"Did you enter the afternoon kindergarten attendance forms?"

"Yep, it's all done. Everyone was here today, which was a surprise. I thought for sure some of the kids would have been absent after the fest yesterday."

"We did have quite a few late students this morning," Nancy remarked.

"I didn't notice with all the major crises that happened all morning long."

"Sorry I didn't come up and say hi at the fest. I saw you were working where the food was, but we went out for a big breakfast beforehand, so Harold and I didn't eat."

"No worries, I didn't even see you there."

"We came mostly to enter the pet costume contest. Sassy dressed as a pirate queen."

Nicole squinted at her co-worker. "You mean you dressed Sassy up as a pirate queen."

"Actually, it was all Harold. He's in a pug parent group on Facebook, and a member posted patterns for Halloween costumes sized for pugs. He downloaded the pattern and worked with Masie's Sewing Shop to bring it to life."

"Oh my gosh! That's so cute! I wish I had seen you guys!"

"Hang on, let me show you the pictures." Nancy put on her readers and pulled up the pictures on her phone.

Nicole leaned over and looked as Nancy thumbed through her pictures.

"Second place! How fun! What was the prize?"

"A growler of our choice from Hop's Heaven and a free grooming from Barkley's Mobile Grooming."

"Very nice. Tell Harold congrats from me."

Nancy looked through her phone again and closed it with a sigh. "Harold loves our little Sassy so much. He takes her with him everywhere, makes her food, and is super involved in the pug parent group. Don't get me wrong, I love our Sassy, but I don't think of her like our child."

"I get that. At the end of the day, Sassy is a dog."

"Right, I just feel bad."

"How so?"

"When I see how devoted he is to Sassy, it makes me think that he would have made such a great dad."

"Oh?" was all Nicole could muster to say.

"We've been married for over thirty years now, and there was a time when we could have pursued why we weren't able to have kids, but I just wasn't built for that. I couldn't handle going through tons of testing and maybe even having surgery. We were happy. We are happy. Harold had always said all he needed was our family of two."

Nicole swallowed hard. Nancy and Harold's many years of marriage had been proof to her you didn't need to have kids to love and be loved and sustain a marriage. Had she been all wrong? Her stomach clenched, and she felt nausea beginning. If Nancy and Harold had regrets, wouldn't Sean as well?

Nancy grabbed a tissue from the box on the counter and dabbed her eyes. "But sometimes, when I see him staring at a dad and his son, he gets this look in his eyes, and I think, 'You did this. You could have tried and maybe Harold would be spoiling a grandkid these days instead of a silly little dog.'"

Nicole gave Nancy a hug. "I'm sorry you feel that way. I'm sure Harold has no regrets." She hoped she was right, and that Harold didn't wish he'd been a father. But the entire conversation was hitting too close to home for her, and she knew all the modern technology in the world could never restore her missing ovaries. She could never give Sean children.

Nicole and Nancy were both quiet for the remainder of the day. Nicole waved goodbye to her coworker and walked home slowly. She'd been waffling about whether to get back to Sean. Talking with Nancy had only confirmed her worst fears. She didn't want to be the one who robbed Sean of having his own kids.

Her stomach sank. Was this what it felt like to love someone enough to let them go? She wanted to be selfish, to call him right now and make plans for him to come over and do everything he did to her the night of the council meeting. She wanted him to take her in his arms and tell her that all he needed was her and that together, they would have a life filled with adventures and love. With enormous effort, she reeled in her wishful thinking. That wasn't the life she was meant to have. He deserved the chance to have a real family. All she could offer him was her companionship. There was no way her company was enough to build a lifetime together.

Chapter Twenty-Three

♥

In a very uncharacteristic move. Sean hadn't set an alarm for Monday morning. After the fest had ended, he'd had to pack up everything and head back to Jesse's Pub. Then all the work of the engagement party after the day at the brewery had almost done him in.

He'd still sent Nicole a quick text before going to bed, and then he'd crawled into bed and slept for a solid twelve hours. When he finally woke up, he checked his phone, anticipating a response from Nicole, only to find no new texts. Maybe his phone needed to refresh. He turned off the Wi-Fi and then turned it back on. Still no text or missed call from Nicole. Well, maybe she'd been busy and hadn't had a chance to reply yet.

He wasn't sure exactly how often people were allowed to text each other when dating, or whatever it was he was doing with Nicole. Then again, he'd never been someone who had to follow the trends. He'd wait until she was probably home from work and give her a call. For now, he had paperwork to do and phone calls to make. Hopefully, that work would keep his mind off Nicole, or perhaps she'd send him a quick reply in the meantime.

At two minutes after four, he decided it was a good time to call Nicole. He knew she was probably home by then and forty-two was his lucky number, so it seemed like a great time to call. He punched in her number and hit send. His heart lurched in his chest with each ring, and his palms were sweaty. The phone rang and rang, then his heart flew into his mouth. "Hello."

"Hey, Nicole."

"Reached Nicole Garrett, I'm unable to take your call right now."

The sweat stopped, and he shivered. Damn, he was really hoping she'd answer. *Beep.*

"H-hey, darling, it's Sean. Just hoping to get a hold of you. I'd like to finish our talk and hear about Devin's emergency. I hope everything is okay. Well, ah, can't wait to talk to you, bye."

Sean hung up the phone. "Hermie, yes, I know that was pretty pathetic. I should have deleted that one and started over! No sense stressing out about it. I'm sure she'll call back soon or send a text. For now, I'll head over to Jesse's and tend my garden."

Within an hour, Sean was putting on his gardening gloves and weeding. Even though it was October, there was still work to do in the garden. He only had another week or two before the temps would dip below freezing. He'd been planning to put up temporary enclosures using PVC pipe and Visqueen to make little semi-permanent greenhouses over his three raised beds.

He took out his tape measure to confirm how long the pipe would need to be to form half circles over the beds. One roll of Visqueen would be plenty. Now he needed to make sure he had a hacksaw to cut the pipes, or maybe he could take them over to Ace Hardware and get them cut to size. That would work.

He hummed a tune as he worked and felt himself slip into his gardening zone. Sean had learned to garden as a kid with his grandfather. He'd found that being in nature, watching plants grow and being responsible for them nurtured his sunny nature. He couldn't live expecting the worst when he had seen a seed grow into a vine that produced dozens of zucchini and tomato plants that provided enough tomatoes to can a gross of salsa. This was the miracle of life that moved him. Seam wondered if Nicole would share his love of gardening. He should have taken a better look at her backyard when he'd been over at her house, but he'd been distracted by her hair, her eyes, and that spectacular ass of hers. Sean shifted a little, thinking back to the night of the council meeting. He craved more of her. The memory of her taste was on his lips, and he had to restrain himself from driving over to her house and knocking on her door.

Once his garden work was complete, he left Jesse's Pub and headed home. He made a simple chicken stir-fry for dinner and then turned on his TV to check out the latest offerings from the streaming channels he subscribed to. He was mindlessly watching TV show previews when his phone rang.

Energy flooded his body, and he rushed into the kitchen to get his phone off the charger. He looked at the display and saw it was his dad. His shoulders dropped, and he decided that as soon as he was done talking to his father he would set a special ringtone for Nicole so he wouldn't get his hopes up anytime someone called him.

"Hey, Dad."

"Hi number one son."

"Is everything okay?"

"What? Do I need a reason to call my son?"

"No, but..."

"Everything is fine. Jenny is great. Hold on a sec. I'll put you on speaker."

Sean groaned internally. He hated being on speakerphone with anyone, but especially with his dad, who always had the TV on in the background.

"Hi Seannie!"

"Hi Jenny." Sean had nothing to say to Jenny, his father's latest wife. Jenny had been around for three years now, but Sean kept his distance. She was his dad's third wife since Sean's mom, and Sean was tired of getting to know the parade of younger wives.

"How's that restaurant of yours?" Jenny asked.

"Going good, going good, thanks for asking."

"Well, you take care, Sean. I'll let you talk to your dad now."

The phone clicked off speakerphone.

"Hey Seannie, I was hoping you could help me with someone."

Ah, Sean thought wryly. His lips turned down. *There's the Dad I know, only calling when he wants something from me. I don't know why I even get my hopes up anymore. The man is like Lucy with the* football, *and I'm Charlie* Brown, *always winding up on my back trying to kick a football that isn't there.*

Sean let out a gigantic sigh and answered his father, "What's going on?"

"Do you remember Ethan?"

"Cindy, wife number two's kid?"

"You don't have to refer to her as wife number two. Don't be crass, Sean."

Sean was glad his father couldn't see his face.

"Sure, I remember him. I babysat him all summer long for three years."

"Oh good. Thing is, he dropped out of college, and he needs some direction in life. I was thinking maybe you could take him in?"

"What?" Sean bellowed.

"Dad, I'm not running a boarding house and I'm not here to be anyone's father."

"Relax, relax, I just thought, since you've been so successful over the past few years, you could share some of that experience with him, help him find some direction, you know, mentor him?"

"Hard pass, Dad. Remember, I live in a studio apartment. I don't have room."

"Well, can you just think about it? What about your friend with the big place, the one you stayed with?"

Sean stared up at the ceiling. His father did not listen when he spoke. He considered just hanging up the phone, but his dad would only call back. Sean sighed.

"Jasper. Dad, I don't think it would work out. I don't even know if Jasper would want another roommate. I'm sure my staying there a few years ago was a one-time thing."

"Sean, Jenny and Ethan don't get along. I can't have him here and it's not like he can go live with his mom, please?"

"Fine, Dad. I'll think about it."

"Oh, wonderful," I'll have Ethan give you a call soon."

Sean tapped his head against the table. Great. Now Ethan was going to call him directly. He was terrible at saying no to any of the kids he helped raise during the summers of his teen years. He hoped the rest of them went off to college or trade school with clear visions and didn't flame out and then come looking for help.

"Bye, Dad."

"Thanks again, Seannie!"

Sean hated that his father was always putting him in positions like this. How could he not help Ethan? He didn't want to feel guilty knowing he might have been able to help one of his step-brothers. What if Ethan got involved with drugs or was depressed? Dang it, he was going to have to try to talk Jasper into letting Ethan stay with him. Unless things worked out with Nicole and he moved in with her, then he'd have no problem subletting to Ethan. "Stop getting ahead of yourself," Sean said out loud. He opened his text messages just in case Nicole had replied and he had missed her text.

Chapter Twenty-Four

Nicole pulled out her bins of Halloween decorations and carried them into the house. Usually, she would have put up everything by October first. This year, she just wasn't feeling it. She opened the bin marked indoor decorations and stared at the ghosts, goblins, and witch decorations practically bursting out of the box. Her shoulders slumped; she wasn't in the mood to hang stuff. She pulled out a pumpkin-shaped pillow and put it on her loveseat. That was enough decorating for one day.

Maybe it was time for her to admit to herself that she was too afraid to take a chance on Sean. She was too afraid to take a chance on anything. Bad things happened when she dreamed. She didn't want to tempt fate. Part of her brain was sure that the moment she gave in and enjoyed life, the cancer would come back. She'd rather go through the motions and take a pension in fifteen years than risk living again.

If she just stayed in her little box and didn't make waves, the horrible specter that was cancer would pass her by. She didn't need a boyfriend or a husband. She was fine all by herself, and fine was fine. It wasn't joyful like Sean's smile when she laughed at his foodie puns. It wasn't that feeling of fluttering butterflies when he kissed her neck. It wasn't that pooling of desire when he slid his hand down and cupped her ass. It was just fine, and she was used to fine.

Nicole finished making her lunch for work and putting out her clothes for Spirit Friday. She looked at her phone as she put it on the charger. She'd spent the week in a fog, going through the motions, barely remembering to eat, and she loved to eat. When her tastebuds started working again after chemo, she'd made it a habit to take her time and savor every bite of her meals. Now those meals tasted like sawdust and cardboard in her mouth.

> SEAN: Nic, I'd really like to talk about us, but if you'd prefer to ghost me, that's your right. My right is not to be jerked around. So, if you want to talk, call me, text me, stop by Jesse's, whatever works. I don't want to bother you. I'm leaving the ball in your court.

She re-read the message again. The door was certainly cracked open. Did she deserve to push it open? Nicole rolled over and punched her pillow a few times. She felt like screaming. She was so tired of life being so hard. The weight of the last few days hung on her, pushing her down into the mattress. She closed her eyes only to find Sean waiting behind them, his arms wide, beckoning her in for a hug.

She woke with a start and rolled over to look at her phone. It was two-thirty in the morning. She'd had that dream again where she was back in the doctor's office, but instead of cancer, she had a benign cyst. Then Duncan showed up to tell her he was moving on because she was broken and he couldn't handle worrying about her. Then she'd looked down and had a baby in her arms. Usually the baby had her face, but today, that baby had Sean's face and then he opened his mouth and started laughing like a hyena. That was when she started screaming in the dream and woke up.

She didn't need to call Zaina to interpret that dream, and she'd been having it for over a year now. At least she'd stopped having the dream where she was back in high school, but she didn't have any clothes on.

She looked over at her phone. *Don't pick it up,* she said to herself, but she didn't listen and soon she was scrolling her fake social media account looking for pictures of Duncan. She hoped for nothing but the worst for him, and she clapped when she saw that his current status was now listed as single. *Good,* she thought. Her face flushed red in the glow of her cell phone. She should be ashamed of herself. She felt like there was a hole where her heart belonged. What was wrong with her?

She was wide awake now and felt a tension headache coming on. Her jaw ached from clenching it all day. She realized she was trying to white-knuckle life, and for what? To lie here at almost three in the morning thinking hateful thoughts about her ex: f she were honest with herself, she could not be any less interested in Duncan if she tried. That tall, broad-shouldered chef with thick dark hair was the elephant in the room.

She wasn't sure what was more painful, staying away from him or opening herself up to potential rejection. She thought it was better for both of them for her to stay away and for him to find someone else, but now she wasn't so sure. Her clarity from the other day was hazy. She wanted to ask Devin or Zaina what they would do, but it didn't matter what they would do. Nicole needed to do what was right for her and for Sean, and she was struggling with that decision.

She got out of bed, went to the kitchen, and made herself a cup of Zaina's sleepy blend tea. The couch beckoned, so she wrapped herself in her favorite blanket and sipped her tea. While she sipped, she made a mental pro and con list. She wished she could talk to Zaina or Devin and have them decide what she should do about Sean, but she felt this was something she must decide on her own. She needed to take all the credit or all the blame. Nicole took out her journal and started listing pros and cons.

> Pro - Sean said he was crazy about her.
> Con - He might decide to leave her someday.
> Pro - The way his eyes crinkled when he smiled at her.
> Con - He loved making food puns.

Who was she kidding? That was a pro, too. In fact, she could list a hundred pros and could only think of one con. And the con was unknowable. They could very well spend the rest of their lives together or just spend the rest of this year. Even Zaina couldn't predict the future. What Nicole could do was continue to keep her head down and go through the motions, alone, and hope she could be lucky enough to live to see her 80s. How would that feel? Would the weight of her regrets slowly grind her down until she was dust? She pulled her blanket around her shoulders like a shawl and took her now empty cup into the kitchen to put it in her sink.

In a perfect world, she'd call her mom right about now, but her parents were on a cruise, so that wasn't a possibility either. She imagined what her mom would have to say. She was certain that both her parents would love Sean. Dad would approve of his well-maintained Jeep and the way he ran a successful business. Mom would say he was very handsome, and she'd love that he had a garden. Both of them would get a kick out of Sean's sense of humor.

As Nicole visualized talking to her parents and imagined seeing them with Sean, she felt her chest swell with pride. When they'd been out together, was proud to be with him. She'd never had that sort of feeling, even when she and Duncan were wedding planning. She never felt secure with Duncan, and maybe that, more than any cancer stuff, is holding her back from going all in with Sean. It was as if a bolt of lightning had hit her. The realization about Duncan knocked her feet out from under her as she plopped back down on the couch.

She laughed out loud. She had been such a fool! "You're a freaking idiot, Nicole!" She shouted. All this time she'd been telling herself she wanted the best for Sean and not to hold him back. Of course, she hadn't bothered to finish their conversation, so she really had no clue what his feelings were about kids—but that wasn't even the real problem! It was all about her fear of being dumped, and that could happen with anyone, anywhere.

She wasn't special. Yes, she literally had scars she was not keen on anyone seeing, but that wasn't what was stopping her. It was the traumatic experience of Duncan that was making her shut down, and she would be damned if she was going to let him stop her from having a chance at happiness with a guy like Sean. That would be bonkers!

She did a little dance around her living room; relief flooded her body, and she felt so happy she thought she might float away. Now all she had to do was show Sean he could count on her, that she trusted him. She looked at the clock on her stove; it was four in the morning.

Her heart was racing. She had so much energy she wanted to run over to see Sean right then and there to tell him she was ready. It was time for her Hallmark moment,...but it was four in the morning, so that would not work. She needed to get some sleep and plan what she was going to say. She knew if she were Sean, she'd have a hard time listening to anything she said after she'd blown him off all week.

Chapter Twenty-Five

♥

Sean was done. He'd been open and honest and shared himself with Nicole. He believed in her and he thought they were on the same page. As for the kids thing, well, he would have told her he'd already spent enough time raising his step-brothers and sisters while his parents went off to find love with new spouses. He'd changed plenty of diapers. He'd even bought tampons for a half-sister and a stepsister, and he'd had to explain wet dreams to a sixth-grade Ethan when he was home from college after junior year.

Rationally, he knew that having kids was more than drudgery. He'd see the happiness of fathers bringing new babies into Jesse's as well as toasting their sons' completion of high school or their daughters getting into law school. He got that, but it wasn't for him.

Sean wanted one life partner; he wanted adventures with someone who had the same values as him and who knew we only got to go around this world once. Sure, he hadn't known

Nicole for very long, but there was something special there. He'd dated in the past, he'd been in love, but he'd never felt like he could make a life with anyone like he felt about Nicole.

Too bad she didn't feel that way about him. After not hearing from her on Monday, he waited until Tuesday afternoon and then he'd sent a quick text, a just checking in message, no blaming, no asking what the heck had happened. This one he didn't even know if she read it or not. The next few days he'd been crazy busy at work training his new sous chef, Lucas. What a welcome distraction that had been, and Lucas had picked up the workflow so well, Sean was thinking he was ready to leave Lucas in charge of brunch on Sunday.

But even training a new right-hand man wasn't enough to keep the thought of Nicole completely out of the forefront of his mind. When he'd ordered a bottle of vanilla to use for waffle batter, he'd thought of her. On his way to work, he'd stopped taking the long way past the lake, so he didn't have to remember the kisses they'd shared after their picnic. He'd been getting coffee from the gas station to avoid Common Grounds. All because of her, she kept showing up in the quiet moments of his day.

Today he couldn't take it any longer, and he sent her a message saying he was giving up. And he was, he was giving up and moving on. That's what he kept telling himself. Yet, here he was, up at four in the morning, unable to sleep. He was thinking about Nicole and missing her. When he inhaled, he could almost convince himself he could smell her scent. If only she were curled up next to him. Nothing could be better than listening to her make little sounds as she slept, to pull her close to him, pushing her hair to the side, and kissing her neck. He reached down and took himself in hand. He needed to get her out of his system, or he was never going to fall back asleep.

Bleary-eyed, he woke up to the drone of his cell phone alarm. Time to face the day. Friday meant happy hour half-off appetizers from two to six, and that guaranteed he would run all day; no time to think about Nicole. Sean had a business to run. He couldn't continue existing in a 'what if' fog. It was time to get on with his life. Plus, he was sure Ethan or his dad would call soon. He needed to talk to Jasper and figure out how he was going to handle that situation. One thing he could always count on his parents for was to remind him why he wasn't a parent himself.

Sean was switching out a keg of Marley Creek Marzen when his phone started vibrating in his pocket. He wasn't in any position to answer the call, no matter who was calling, so he let it go to voicemail. He promptly got involved with one minor issue after another. Thank goodness Lucas was here to help with the cooking because they were slammed. They ran out of salmon twenty minutes into the dinner service, and then the point of sale was down for the last two hours, and he'd had Mable use the app on his phone to process all the credit cards. Finally, the last patrons were leaving, and it was time to clean up.

"You're quiet today, boss," Mable said. She was sitting at the bar, rolling silverware for tomorrow's brunch. Her blonde hair had recently been streaked with purple and was in a French braid.

"When did you add the purple to your hair?"

"At least a week ago. You just noticed?" She tossed her hair

"I guess I did." He yawned loudly.

"Boss, you have some major bags under those eyes." Sean finished organizing the bar for the next day, and then he walked around the bar and sat down next to Mable.

"I haven't been able to sleep for shit this week."

"You must really be exhausted, Sean. You're swearing in my presence. I am shocked."

"Geez, I didn't even realize I did that. I'm sorry. I've been distracted all week, and it's not acceptable."

"I think you should cut yourself some slack, Sean. Even when you aren't your sunny, organized self, you are still a talented chef, and we had a great night."

"We did run out of that salmon right off the bat."

"True, and that's only because we have people coming back just to have it. Our salmon's got its own word of mouth going on at this point. You should be really proud of that."

Sean felt warmth rising in his chest and up his neck. "Thanks Mable. I appreciate that. Sometimes I get lost in the weeds and don't stop to savor our successes."

"Man, it's all you, boss."

"Ah, stop, Mable, what would I do without you?"

Mable cocked her head, thinking. "I'm sure you'd manage. Don't get too used to me. I only have a year left of grad school, then I'm off to get a real job."

"That will be a sad day indeed," he said, shaking his head slowly.

"Don't worry, I'll help find my replacement. Now tell me what's going on with Nicole," Mable crossed her arms and gave Sean a stern look.

"I hate when I forget that you're a psych major."

"Actually, one day I'll be a school psychologist."

"Tomatoes, toe-mah-toes."

"What's the scoop? I thought all was well?"

"I think she ghosted me, and I just need to get over it."

Sean explained how they had worked together at the fest and how he'd called and messaged, but Nicole hadn't returned any contact with him.

"What do you think? Is there anything else I can do?"

Mable patted Sean's arm, "I'm sorry, that really sucks. I mean, this is why I barely date. Who needs the bullshit? I'd rather focus on school. Someday when I've got my degree and a job with benefits, then maybe I'll work on finding some true love."

Sean sighed and rubbed at a spot on the bar with his thumb. "If it were only that easy."

Mable got up and patted Sean on the shoulder, "Sorry boss man, love stinks."

Sean shrugged his shoulders, "I guess. You've still helped me. I'm gonna stop having hope that there is something I should have done or should have said that would make Nicole call me or text me and tell me she was sorry and then we could live happily ever after. It's better for me to not have hope, so I can move on and stop thinking about her."

Mable threw her arms around Sean, "It'll be okay."

He gave her a one-armed hug back. "Thanks, Mab, go ahead and get out of here. It's the weekend and I know you are off tomorrow. Enjoy your Friday night."

"Thanks so much!" Mable bounded out of the dining room and into the kitchen to grab her coat, and within seconds, she was out the door.

Sean walked through the restaurant, making sure everything was set for tomorrow's brunch. He put on his jacket and paused at the front door for a moment, looking at Jesse's Pub to remind himself of the business he'd built in only a few short years. He had so much going for him. His personal life would catch up with him, and one day he'd have a partner to share this.

Maybe what he had with Nicole should show him it was worth getting back out there dating again. He headed home, feeling much lighter than he had in days. His nature was to see the good things in others and himself, and for the last few days he'd been in a real funk, not believing in himself and feeling cynical about relationships. In fact, if Nicole came into Jesse's tomorrow, it wouldn't bother him at all. He'd be happy to see her as a friend. Yep, that's what he was going to keep telling himself until it was true. *Fake it 'til you make it, Sean!*

Chapter Twenty-Six

♥

Nicole sat at her kitchen table and ate the veggie sandwich she had put together. When you have cancer, it's all about surviving the day, getting through treatment. She thought back to those hard, hard days. The nurses had been so helpful, providing tips for avoiding nausea, what lotions to use for radiation, but no one prepared you for life after treatment. She wished she had someone to talk with about intimacy after lumpectomy and radiation. She needed someone to tell her that her body was good enough.

She ate a few potato chips and pondered. Could Sean be that person? She wished she didn't have any of this to worry about. If only she hadn't had breast cancer, then she could take off her shirt, or not even bother with a bra, or heck, she could sleep naked. Although if she hadn't had cancer, she'd be married to Duncan and maybe even had kids with him. An involuntary shudder went through her at the thought. Perhaps that alternative reality would be even worse than what happened in this one. She might have a child, but he'd probably leave her in that reality for someone else when he had to deal with her postpartum.

She just wanted to have some positive feedback before she let Sean see her topless. It was going to be awkward enough going over to Sean's and baring herself literally and figuratively to him. She needed someone she trusted to see what she had going on and tell her if she looked hideous or not. She couldn't tell. All the confidence she'd had in her body was lost the day she felt that lump.

She shouted, "That's it!" She'd ask Devin. Devin would tell her if her worries were founded or unfounded, and most importantly, she wouldn't think Nicole was crazy for asking her to look at her boobs.

Nicole sent a quick text to Devin:

> NIC: Can I come over tonight, after the twins are down? I need your help with something. It won't take long.

> DEV: Of course! Does eight work?

> NIC: Perfect, see you then!

Nicole flopped back in her chair, relieved and nervous.

Promptly at eight o'clock, Nicole texted Devin from Devin's driveway. She knew better than to knock or ring the doorbell. If she caused the twins to wake up, Devin would kill her. Once she received the all-clear from Devin, she walked up to the expansive two-story brick home Devin called her McMansion. The porch was cheerfully decorated with a bale of hay, pumpkins, and a smiling scarecrow.

Nicole quietly let herself in and walked into the kitchen where Devin was sitting in her pajamas and wearing fuzzy slippers. She had a bottle of red wine open and two glasses set out. Devin gestured for Nicole to sit down at the marble-topped island, and then she poured each of them a glass of wine. They both clinked their glasses and took a drink.

Devin spoke first, "So, what's going on?"

"You might think I'm crazy, but here goes. I'm here because you are a most trusted friend and probably the only person in the world I feel comfortable sharing this with." She could feel her face turning flaming red, so she placed a palm on each cheek, trying to cool them down.

Devin nodded. "Whatever it is, it warms my heart to know you feel like you can tell me anything. I know sometimes people are intimidated by me, and I'd hate for that to be the case with us."

Nicole reached over and gripped her friend's hand. "Okay, I'm ready," she said.

Devin took her other hand and gave it a squeeze. "What's going on, hon?"

Nicole pulled back her hands and held them in her lap. She began speaking about those last days with Duncan, and how much was taken away from her, and how much it had hurt to lose the simple confidence she'd always had in her body.

She took a proffered tissue from Devin and wiped her eyes, "It's not like I ever thought I had an amazing body or anything, but I'd always had faith that it was healthy and that if it wasn't healthy that I'd know something was wrong. But I didn't; I had no clue. My boobs were trying to kill me, and I was planning a wedding."

Devin kept steady eye contact with Nicole as she spoke. "I don't expect you or anyone else to understand what I went through, and how devastating it was and it is for me. I am broken," she said shakily, feeling numbness setting in as she spoke.

Tears were flowing down Devin's face. She got up and poured a couple of glasses of water and set them down. She took a long drink and then she spoke. "I'm so sorry that you feel less-than. I won't say broken because I don't believe that for a second."

"Thank you," Nicole said through her tears. "I'm telling you all this not to be sad for me, but I actually wanted to see if you'd look at my boobs."

Devin burst out with a laugh and then covered her mouth and looked at Nicole wide-eyed. "Ah, why?"

Nicole's eyes were bright now with mischief instead of tears. "I know," she nodded. "It sounds ridiculous, but hear me out." She held up a finger. "One, if you see me topless, then Sean isn't the first and only person to see me without a shirt on in over five years—excluding all the random medical professionals who have, of course. Basically, I need this for my ego," she joked. "Two, I know you'll give me your honest, unvarnished opinion, and that way, I won't have any unpleasant surprises when Sean sees me."

Devin replied, "I can be honest, but I'm not unbiased. I think you are beautiful from head to toe. Seeing you topless won't change that, wouldn't change that even if you'd decided to have both of them removed. I know it's a trite old phrase, you are beautiful inside and out—so I'll say instead that your boobs don't define you, and besides whenever I've seen you with him, that man is looking at your butt."

Nicole walked around the table and hugged Devin. Her heart felt full with the words Devin had just spoken, but she still needed visual confirmation that she wasn't hideous.

"Before we do this thing, I just want to point out how proud I am of you for taking a chance on another man. I know the last few years have been just awful, and I'm in awe of how you kept pushing through the disappointments and all the pain. Especially when you made the decision to lose your ovaries. It just stinks you had to make that decision before you'd had a chance to have kids."

Nicole let out an enormous sigh and slumped in her chair. Not being able to have kids was heartbreaking, even more so because it was something else cancer had taken away from her. She hadn't spent a lot of time, as a kid or an adult, dreaming of the day she'd become a mother, but that didn't mean it wasn't something she wanted for herself. Her voice was low with emotion, "Thank you, Devin. Some days have been so hard." She took a few moments to gather herself, and then she rallied, determined to continue her mission.

"Now that we've gotten that out of the way," Nicole said as Devin blew her a kiss. "Are you ready to check out my boobs?"

"Honey, I've been ready," Devin joked in a sultry tone.

"Behave," Nicole playfully swatted Devin's arm.

Devin got up. "Let's go back to the guest room so we aren't standing in front of a window. We sure don't want Old Man Stevens getting an eyeful."

"Old Man Stevens?"

Devin waved her hand. "Doesn't exist. I just made it up."

"You scared me there for a second," Nicole said.

"This is such an unusual situation. I can't decide if this is just no big deal, or if we should do shots first, or if I should offer you a robe? It's your call. How can I make you comfortable?" The guest bedroom was painted light green and had a full bed with a blue comforter. The bed was oak, and there was a long oak dresser with a large mirror. One feature Devin had demanded when this house was built was that each bedroom had an ensuite bath. Devin opened the top dresser drawer and pulled out a short terry cloth robe. "Would you like this?"

Nicole took the robe. "I have to say, for me, it's kind of a big deal. Shots on a weeknight are a big no, and thanks very much for the robe." She walked into the bathroom and shut the door. She set down the robe on the counter. Her mouth was dry. She wondered if it was this hard to have no shirt on in front of someone she'd known and loved for practically three decades, how was it going to feel to take off her top in front of Sean? She shouldn't try to do this. Maybe she'd feel more comfortable in a few months, or maybe he would mind. Maybe they could have sex with their clothes on? Hey it happened on TV fairly often.

"You can do hard things," Devin said from the bedroom, as if she understood Nicole's current mindset.

Nicole took a deep breath, rubbed the sweat off her hands on her jeans, and then she took off her shirt and bra and slipped into the robe. She cinched it closed, put her hand on the door handle, and opened the door. Then she walked over to Devin, shut her eyes, and opened the robe.

"I think I'm having breast surgeon PTSD," she said nervously.

"Don't worry," said Devin, "I'm only going to look. I won't touch you or check for any lumps."

Nicole shivered, "Ugh, definitely a PTSD moment."

"Honey, you look fine. You look like a woman in her thirties, with a nice rack."

"But the one?"

"It just looks like it needs a little attention. Let's say you were in a crowd of topless women, you wouldn't stand out. I mean, if it would make you feel better, I'd show you what I look like after tandem breast-feeding the twins for a year. We've been through some life-altering things, Nicole, and our bodies only tell part of that story. I'm not saying it's all in your head. I'm saying you've still got them, and you shouldn't be afraid to flaunt them."

"I'm trying to roll my eyes at that last part, but my eyes are too puffy from crying." Nicole tied the robe and sat down next to Devin on the bed.

"You have a terrible time taking compliments, but I need you to accept this one. You are a beautiful, amazing woman."

Nicole just smiled, her throat and heart too full to speak.

"I'm not always right."

Nicole cocked her head and smiled, "Big of you to say."

Devin gently knocked her knee into Nicole's leg. "Behave, I'm trying to hype you up. Sean likes you and I am sure that he will be elated that you are ready to show all of yourself to him and I know he will worship you like the goddess you are. I see your face, I know you want to pooh-pooh this, and I need you to stop."

Nicole squished her mouth shut and went back to the bathroom to change. When she came out, Devin was back in the kitchen hand-washing their glasses. Nicole walked over and gave her friend a hug. "Thank you so much. I don't know what I'd do without you," Nicole whispered into Devin's hair.

"This is what friends are for," Devin said, rubbing Nicole's back.

"I'll let you know what happens with Sean."

"You better," Devin said, and she walked Nicole to the door.

Chapter Twenty-Seven

♥

Sean was back at work for another weekend brunch. Why had he started doing these dumb brunches in the first place? He could be at home right now, sleeping. Instead, he was running around the kitchen trying to find the bagel slicer. He hadn't done bagels at brunch before, but Donnie from Books and Bagels had called yesterday and offered him a fantastic deal on an overstock of pumpkin bagels he had made for an event. Now he had four dozen bagels and no bagel slicer to be found. He really should have asked Donnie to slice them. "This is what happens when you don't get enough sleep," he mumbled under his breath.

On top of that, he was short-staffed and couldn't spare anyone to stand and cut the bagels. He pulled out a cutting board and a serrated knife. He hated to do it, but the fastest thing to do was cut all the bagels in half instead of cutting them through. It was that or not cut them at all, and whole bagels would be a hassle for his guests.

By the time he was done, he had a cramp in his hand, but at least he could get them out to the buffet. If he'd been running on all cylinders, he would have made some nice honey butter, or had a bagel slicer and a toaster on the buffet, but he had none of that. He hated feeling unprofessional and disorganized. *This is all her fault.* His heart immediately ached. What was the sense in thinking anything like that? As much as he'd like to blame Nicole for everything, that was a little too dramatic for him. He was sure that if he could just get a good night's sleep, he wouldn't be so grumpy anymore.

He carried the chafing dish piled high with pumpkin bagel halves out to the dining room and added them to the far end of the buffet. There were already a few people lined up at the door waiting for Mable to unlock it. He regretted his complaining about the weekend brunch service. It was foolish to moan about his business being successful, especially when so many restaurants didn't make it past their first year. It wasn't like him to forget to be grateful.

"Now don't fill up on these bagels, Mrs. Woodsman. I've got some eggs so fresh the hens still think they are sitting on them."

The bespectacled elderly lady asked, "Are these from Donnie's shop?"

"Yes, ma'am."

"Well then, I'll just have one of these and skip my usual plum Danish. Then I'll have room for a nice little Swiss cheese and mushroom omelet." She added a big smear of cream cheese to her plate and continued on her way.

Sean returned to his place behind the portable burners and double-checked to make sure he had an extra canister of propane so he would be prepared if he ran out of firepower.

Yesterday he'd been catering the Marley Creek Men's Club's monthly breakfast, when he'd been so distracted by his thoughts of Nicole that he'd run out of propane and stood there for what seemed like an eternity waiting for an egg to cook while a white-haired gentleman glowered at him.

Nicole was messing with his head, and he wasn't sure how to make it stop. Sean frowned and barked, "Next," to the line of people, and a little old lady, probably someone who was friends with Mrs. Woodsman, jumped in fright. He stopped what he was doing, turned off his burners, and walked over to the woman. He mentally facepalmed and then spoke to her.

"Ma'am, I'm so sorry I startled you. I'm Sean, the owner of Jesse's. Please accept my apology and to make it up to you, your meal is on the house today."

The woman looked up at him. She placed her gnarled hand in his and he shook it gently, in case her arthritis was bothering her. She smiled and her entire face crinkled. "Thank you so much. I'd really appreciate it. Any chance I can get a doggy bag, too? My little Maxine loves sausage."

Sean smiled. He admired the old woman's nerve. He was often telling himself, don't ask, don't get. In fact, that philosophy was the genesis of this problem named Nicole. "Where are you sitting? I'll have someone bring over a to-go box of sausage and bacon for your pup."

She shook Sean's hand firmly and said, "That's so kind of you, and as long as your food tastes as good as your customer service, I will give you a five-star rating."

Sean smiled and laughed wide enough that you could see all of his teeth. "Thank you, madam!" he said and went back behind the burners. "Now, what do you want in your omelet?"

By the time brunch was over, all the pumpkin bagels were long gone, and so were the new eggs. He hoped his new local supplier of free-range eggs could keep up with the demand. He made a note to see if they had any recommendations if they couldn't provide enough eggs. Soon it would be time for holiday brunches, and he knew he would be packed.

As he cleaned up from the busy morning, he gave himself a pat on the back for keeping the thinking about Nicole to a minimum. They'd only gone out a few times, and yet she had such a hold on him. Maybe, he thought, maybe he should reach out to her one more time.

He started to take out his phone, and then he recovered his senses. Nope, he'd called and texted several times, and the last text made it clear that if there was any interest on her part, Nicole needed to contact him. He needed to back off in case she just needed time to process some issues of her own. He couldn't do anything else, and that was the problem.

Sean was a can-do guy, and he knew he could fix whatever the problem was if she would let him, but that wasn't the right thing to do. Not much bothered him more than having to sit on his hands and let things play out, but at this point that was his only hope. He pulled the grates off the stove and picked up a Brillo pad. He might as well get his frustrations out cleaning.

They didn't have any private parties, and the big college football matchups were noon games. The Saturday night crowd was quiet, and they were closed for the night by eight. He was stopped at the main stoplight in town when he heard his phone ping in his back pocket. Even though the streets were basically empty on this gloomy October night, he decided whoever was texting him could wait until he got home.

His feet ached as he dragged himself up the two flights of stairs to his third-floor apartment, walked into his place and headed straight for the shower. As much as he loved the smell of bacon, it had been a long, long day and he wanted to feel clean, and he wanted to hit the sack. Once the hot water was turned on, he shucked off his clothes. He was putting them in the hamper when his phone fell out of his pants and clattered to the floor. He picked it up and turned it over to check whether the screen had broken in the fall. His screen was intact, and there was a notification. He clicked the text icon and saw a new text from Nicole. His legs almost gave way, and he plopped down onto the toilet. Was she texting to tell him to buzz off, or did she miss him like he missed her?

> NICOLE: Hi Sean, I'm sorry for being such a jerk. Can you give me a chance to explain myself to you? Or is it too late?

Sean wiped the steam off his phone and re-read the text five times, then replied.

Sean began writing, not to late. Then he corrected it, not too late. Then he deleted the entire message. He put his phone down and got in the shower. Then he backed away from the shower curtain and picked up his phone again.

Sean typed:

> SEAN: Thanks for admitting you were being a jerk. It's not too late. What did you have in mind?

Then he deleted that and finally decided on:

> SEAN: I don't think it's too late. When would you like to talk?

He hit send and made himself get in the shower so he wouldn't spend the next however many minutes sitting in a steam-filled bathroom wasting hot water and hoping she would text him back or call. After a very short shower, he wrapped a towel around his waist and turned on the exhaust fan so he could see his phone. She had replied!

> NICOLE: Are you free now?

Talk about your second wind; Sean felt like he'd just had a triple espresso. He pulled out his electric razor and his favorite body lotion, the one that smelled like sandalwood and citrus.

> SEAN: Yes, I can swing by in about half an hour.

He waited as three dots bubbled next to her name.

> NICOLE: Sounds great!

Sean fist-pumped and did a little dance in his bathroom, then he finished primping and was out the door. *What was she going to say?* He wanted to believe that Nicole missed him as much as he missed her. Maybe not as much as he missed her, but well, at least she wanted to see him. That must mean she missed him.

Butterflies filled his stomach, and he could feel his heart in his throat as he drove to her house. In his joy at being invited over to Nicole's, there was a kernel of resentment. He didn't want to be in a relationship with someone who was not all in with him. He hoped she understood this was it.

Chapter Twenty-Eight

♥

Nicole woke up on Saturday morning and turned on her October playlist. She opened up the bin of Halloween decorations and began decorating. So many of the decorations were from fun times she'd had with Devin and Zaina. She put out her witchy mugs and the plug-in cauldron that was an oil warmer, and soon her little home smelled and looked like the season. The weight of last week had lifted, and she swore if she weighed herself, she'd weigh ten pounds less.

Once she had her home just the way she wanted it, she sat down with a cup of pumpkin spice-flavored coffee and her journal. She thought better when she wrote things out. Nicole took her favorite pen and began figuring out what to text Sean. She briefly thought about calling him, but she was afraid the words would get stuck in her throat.

An hour later the coffee was long gone, and she'd written and crossed out three pages of texts to send to Sean. Maybe she should just call him? Her throat started to close; no, she definitely needed to text him. She crumpled up the papers and threw them into the recycling bin. It was a beautiful, sunny mid-October day, and she decided to go for a walk and then she'd tackle that text.

She put on her favorite pair of sneakers and threw on a sweatshirt and headed out the door. She took a deep breath and smelled fall in the air. Leaves crunched under her feet as she walked, and she relished the wind pushing her hair back. Sunlight filtered through the maple trees that lined the block, and as the breeze blew, golden leaves fell to the ground like the first snow.

She practiced being in the moment and enjoying the world around her. Nicole walked with her head up and her shoulders straight, making eye contact with people she passed. She even said hello and smiled at a few people. This was her place, and this was her time. When she turned the corner back onto her street, she admired her house from afar. If all went well, Sean could help her with the outside decorations. If he had time, he could even help her give out candy to the trick-or-treaters after school. She pictured Sean and herself sitting at the bistro table she had placed on the small patio next to her door.

For the first time in a very long time, daydreaming about a future didn't make her sad or anxious. Joy bubbled up inside her. Was she finally going to follow through on her promise to herself and let go of worrying about whether cancer would come back one day? Even as she let that tiny hope get a foothold in her brain, she knew, even with Sean at her side, there would be days where the fears would win out and she'd be afraid to allow herself to be happy. But what would life with Sean and her be like? Could she see that possibility becoming a reality?

She strolled up to her front door and sat on the patio. It was time to practice some Mindfulness-Based Stress Reduction for the first time in months. She'd learned the technique for anxiety reduction by taking a class at the Marley Creek Library. When she felt centered, she picked up her phone and texted Sean. *Whoosh* went the text, and now she would wait and see if he responded.

When she thought back to their time together, she honestly wasn't sure if he would reply to her text. Would she? Perhaps? The worry that he might not reply or want to see her again couldn't overcome her pride at putting herself out there. She told herself that even if he didn't want to see her again, that was okay too. The point was that she was scared, but she did it anyway. She could hold her head high, and if she happened to run into him somewhere in town, she'd smile and say hello. *Maybe they could even be friends,* she told herself. Her stomach flip-flopped in response. Well maybe not friends, but she would certainly be cordial and try not to think about Sean with his shirt off.

She kept herself busy throughout the afternoon. For dinner, she decided it was a good day to make vegetable soup and fresh bread. She went online and found a no-knead bread recipe she could make in her Dutch oven, and while the bread was rising; she rummaged through her fridge and cabinets for vegetables for her soup. She had plenty of celery, carrots, and onions to start with, and then she found a bag of frozen cauliflower, peas, and a can of corn in her cabinet.

Soon the soup was simmering on the stove. She put the soup on low and placed the bread in the oven. Once a timer was set, she sat on her couch. She bit her lip. Time was passing like molasses, and checking her phone constantly wasn't helping. She'd been starving when she'd started cooking, but now that it was cooking and she had time to think about Sean, she wasn't hungry at all.

It had only been a couple of hours since she sent her text. Again, she double-checked her phone, just to make sure she had sent the text. She had, and it said "Delivered." He was probably busy at the restaurant. Nicole ran a hand through her hair and twisted the ends between her fingers. Why she thought he'd reply quickly to her text was beyond her. Maybe he didn't look at his phone until he was done working for the day.

She scrolled up to Zaina's contact information in her phone and dialed her number.

The phone rang four times and then went to voicemail. Nicole hung up. Zaina was probably busy with a customer. Finally, the timer went off. Her soup and bread were done. She ladled herself a bowl, glad that her appetite had returned at the sight of the colorful soup and the freshly baked bread. She pulled off a hunk of bread and spread butter on it. The butter quickly melted, and she took a big bite. "Yum," she said. Then she sat down with her dinner and turned on the TV to see if there were any good movies to watch.

She finished her food and lay down to continue watching TV. The fresh air and the hearty meal made her eyes droopy, and she decided she would treat herself to a little late afternoon nap. Two hours later, she woke up. *Well, that definitely was going to make it tough to sleep tonight.*

She stretched, reaching up to the sky, then down to touch her toes, then she plopped back down on the couch and rubbed her temples. How was it only seven? This day had gone on for at least a decade. She needed to find something to do to pass the time.

Her phone buzzed, and she grabbed it like a drowning man grabbing an oar. Zaina's face flashed on the screen. Her heartbeat ratcheted down, and she swiped to take the call.

"Hey, Zaina," Nicole said.

"Hi, Nic. I saw you called. What's up?"

"Are you busy at the shop? I don't want to keep you from customers."

"No, I'm upstairs. I close at six on Saturday."

"Okay, great." Nicole felt suddenly nervous.

"What's going on?"

"You didn't see my text in the group chat?"

"The shop was surprisingly busy today. I just saw the missed call and called you back," Zaina stifled a yawn.

"I sent Sean a text," Nicole said shyly.

"You didn't!"

"Yep, I did." Her voice sounded stronger now.

"What did you say?"

"Just that I was sorry and could we get together and talk."

"Nicole, that's awesome! I really think he's the guy for you!" Zaina said confidently.

"I guess we will see. Now I'm driving myself bonkers, hoping he'll reply."

"Yeah, that sucks. Hmm, what's a good distraction?" Nicole could hear Zaina tapping her nails against a table.

"I'll try anything."

"Wait! I've got it! Watching animals doing funny stuff on your phone! Every time I do that, I think only ten minutes has passed, but it'll turn out I've been on my phone for like an hour."

"I guess I'll try it. I'm dying over here; the waiting is terrible. I hope he texts me back tonight and puts me out of my misery. Don't look at me like that."

"How do you know I'm looking at you like that? We aren't on FaceTime."

"Please, how long have we been friends? I know you are giving me a look that's saying, you are experiencing the consequences of your own actions, silly woman!"

"Okay, I am, and you are," Zaina said in a singsong voice.

"True, and I deserve it. Ugh, I've been an unmitigated ass."

"Yes, you have. Fortunately, I'm pretty sure Sean is the type to forgive you."

"God, I hope so." Nicole let out a sigh.

"It's gonna work out, Nicole."

"Thanks Z, I really appreciate the pep talk."

"Anytime, Nic! That's what best friends are for."

"Love you."

"Love you too! Now go watch some videos and stop stressing out!" Zaina commanded.

"Bye!" Nicole sighed. Well, at least it was now seven-thirty. She figured that if Sean looked at her text tonight, it probably wouldn't be until after he was done at work, probably not until nine or ten. *Oh no,* she thought, *what if he sees it and thinks it's too late to text and he waits until* tomorrow? *Ugh!* She threw a throw pillow across the room.

She put away the leftover soup and bread, and then began watching funny animal videos. She was surprised how many videos featured bears. Nicole was watching the fourth in a series of videos involving bears showing up on people's ring cameras when a text notification popped up from Sean. Her heart pounded in her ears, and warmth flooded her body. This was it. Her hand was shaking as she opened the text.

She read it once, then she read it again and did a dance around her living room. He wanted to come over! She knew that he'd probably had a long day at the restaurant and that he didn't have to work on Monday, so maybe she should suggest they get together tomorrow night.

She began typing:

> NICOLE: Are you free tomorrow night?

Her finger hovered over the send button. She couldn't do it. She had to go for broke and see if he could come over tonight, preferably like right now.

> NICOLE: Are you free now?

She hit send and let out a huge breath of air. *If he's not free tonight, that's okay. It'll be fine,* she reassured herself. Then she could ask him if he was available tomorrow afternoon.

"I can be by in half an hour," she read aloud then blurted out, "Oh my God, oh my God, oh my God!" Nicole jumped up and down as her brain short-circuited.

> NICOLE: Sounds great!

She typed back and then made a mad dash to freshen up and change her clothes.

Chapter Twenty-Nine

♥

Sean knocked on Nicole's door. He remembered how nervous he'd been when he first came to her house. Today, that nervousness was amped up. He chewed the inside of his cheek. Maybe he was a little apprehensive as well. He realized he'd forgotten to eat dinner in his excitement, and now he felt a little queasy.

He waited for Nicole to answer the door. With each hour-long second that passed, the more sweat broke out. A sheen of sweat started at his forehead and now covered the rest of his face. He patted his pockets, looking for anything to wipe the sweat off. He found a receipt from a grocery trip and was using that to blot his face when she opened the door. Her smile took his breath away.

"Thank you for coming over," she stood back and opened the door wide for him to enter.

She shut the door behind him as he walked through.

He toed off his shoes. Nicole's hair was in soft waves framing her face. She must have gotten a new lipstick because her lips were the color of raspberries, his favorite berries. He looked at her and waited for her to make the next move.

"Can I get you something to drink?" She rubbed her hands on her pants. He could see her pulse beating in the hollow between her collarbones.

"That would be nice. What do you have?" He had a sudden strong desire to do anything he could to make her comfortable. He bit the inside of his lip and stopped himself from saying, "Relax, Nicole." He knew no one liked to be told to relax.

"I have some red wine, or water? Or I could make tea?"

On the kitchen counter, there was a bottle of wine and a couple of glasses. "A glass of wine sounds good."

"Great, I'll go get us the wine." Nicole turned to go to the kitchen and then turned back. She waved her hand. She had on black nail polish. He loved when women wore black nail polish. "Sit wherever you'd like."

Sean looked around and decided on the loveseat. He hoped she'd sit next to him and not sit in the recliner. Sean tried to stifle a yawn. The day had been long, and his sleep had been awful. Nicole was pouring the wine and missed seeing his valiant attempt not to yawn.

She walked into the room and set the wineglasses on the coffee table. She stood for a second longer and then sat next to Sean. His inner self did a cartwheel. He breathed in her scent, and it grounded him after a long, stressful day. His longing for her made his chest ache. How he wanted her in his life!

"Should we toast?" Nicole asked, giving him a darting glance.

"What would you like to toast?" he asked quietly.

She tilted her head, and it was all he could do to stop from leaning over and kissing her neck. He shifted slightly as his pants strained.

She brought her glass close to his. "To a new beginning?"

He clinked his glass against hers and said, "Tell me more."

They both took a drink, and Nicole set her glass back on the table. Sean kept his glass and leaned back, getting comfortable on the loveseat. He was ready to listen to anything and everything Nicole had to say.

"A few years ago," she began, "I was engaged. We were in the midst of wedding planning when I found a lump in the shower."

"Oh, Nicole," he said, his throat thick. "Is this what you mentioned when we were at Common Grounds? It was cancer, wasn't it?"

Nicole's eyes were glossy with tears; she sniffed. Sean's heart ached for her, and he fumbled in his pocket, pulled out his receipt and handed it to Nicole. "Here," he said.

She took the receipt. "Um?" Her brow furrowed.

"I panicked. I wanted to give you a tissue, but all I had on me was this receipt."

She smiled and her cheeks flushed. "That's so sweet of you. Can I give you a hug?"

"Always. Remember, I'm a hugger." She moved closer to him and hugged him hard. He rubbed her back, and then he smoothed back her hair and kissed her forehead. He held her for a moment, listening to her heartbeat and waited for her to continue.

"Yes, it was cancer, and it was the aggressive kind where you definitely have to have chemo plus radiation."

"I'm sorry, I don't even know what to say." His eyes were stinging with tears.

"It's okay. I get that. If it weren't me, I wouldn't know what to say either. Plus, it's even worse when you're young. Like, how the heck could I have cancer? I was only thirty-three."

"That must have been such a shock."

"And because I was young for breast cancer, I got genetic testing." Her voice quavered.

Sean was quiet and let her continue.

She paused for a moment, her breathing shaky, and he reached over and began slowly her arms.

"I have the BRCA-1 gene, and that puts me at a pretty high risk of ovarian cancer. I spent months going through all these horrible cancer treatments, and I couldn't handle the thought of another cancer showing up and having to go through everything again. Especially if there was any way I could avoid it."

"What a nightmare."

"Tell me about it," she clenched her hands together, "it was a super hard decision. If I didn't already have cancer, I would have made a different decision, but that wasn't my reality. I decided to have preventive surgery so I would not have to worry about ovarian cancer. The giant downside of course..." She paused, and he nodded his head.

"This is what you were talking about at the fest. Why you said you can't have kids. Oh, Nicole." His heart ached for her. His brown eyes filled with tears.

She nodded. Her tears had dried now.

"You're so brave," Sean took her hands in his and looked her in the eyes. She didn't meet his eyes as she began talking.

"Before you say anything," she began, "I need to make this clear. You may say that you don't want to have kids, and that it's a non-issue. I'll be happy to hear that. But one day we might be together and you might change your mind. You're younger than me."

Sean couldn't stop himself from slowly shaking his head no.

Nicole smiled slightly. "The point is, I finally understand, everything has risks. I've been so focused on trying to make sure I never have cancer again that I forgot about the risks worth taking. Nothing is a sure thing, but if I'm not willing to risk my heart for you, then what's the point? Then the only guarantee I have in life is that I'll never have you."

Nicole looked into his eyes, and he felt the warmth of her lock suffuse his whole body.

She took a deep breath and continued, "I made a promise to myself that if you were willing to come here and listen to me, that I'd risk it all for you. I love you, Sean Harper."

Sean's heart beat out of his chest. He pulled her to him and crushed his lips against hers.. She moaned a little, and his tongue slid into her mouth. He wanted to taste her every day for the rest of his life. They kissed harder, and he wanted to be deep inside her. He reached up and caressed her cheek. He pulled away, and she was panting; her eyes were on fire.

He put his forehead against hers, "I love you too," he said, stunned by the amazing turn of events this day had taken. He pulled her into his lap and began nibbling on her earlobe.

"That feels so good," she said, and he rocked her against his jeans.

Chapter Thirty

♥

Her life had been a runaway train the last few years, and finally it felt like she was on the right track. But now she was on a roller coaster, slowly inching up to the top of the mountain. She took a deep breath and put his hand on her button-down shirt. Nicole placed his fingers on the first button and they undid it together. She was straddling his lap in a pair of thin loungewear pants. His arousal pressed against her own growing wetness. She ran her hands through his hair as he slowly unbuttoned her shirt.

She enjoyed her position of control over him, feeling powerful in a way she had never felt before. She was in charge. He loved her. Flutters filled her chest as he reached for the last button. Her opened shirt exposed her lacy black bra. She shrugged off her shirt and flung it onto a chair. She looked down at herself and then looked at Sean. His eyes were focused on her lacy bra.

The cup on the right was filled fully, but the cup on the left was only filled halfway at best. He reached tentatively for her left breast. She stilled as he slowly rubbed the lace. Her nipple stood at a peak, and the rough feel of the lace only enhanced her desire. She moaned a little as he pulled gently.

He kept his hand on her breast and he leaned in, kissing along her collarbone as he slowly made his was down to her breast. He kissed her over the bra, lightly teasing her nipple with his teeth. She ran her hands through his hair as he worked. She rocked slowly, letting him attend to her a while longer. Then, when she felt ready, she tapped his shoulder. He stopped and looked up at her. She undid her bra and tossed it with her shirt.

Sean's eyes were enormous as he took her all in. He carefully traced a small scar on the far side of her breast with his thumb, gently caressing it. She nodded, and he leaned forward and softly kissed the line of her scar. He began kneading her right breast while he continued to lavish attention on her broken breast. He took it into his mouth. His tongue swirled around her nipple, lightly flicking it. She ran her fingers through his hair and looked down at him. She was rocking harder against him now. Her lips were feeling engorged as they rubbed against his zipper. He paused for a moment, breathing air onto her heated breast. Then he went to work on the other side, repeating the process. She felt so full of desire, and feeling desired that she thought joy would burst through every fiber of her being.

"You are so beautiful." He said, his voice husky.

Her eyes were glossy again, as tears welled up. She was so grateful she had taken this risk. She pushed up Sean's shirt, taking her hands and running them over his abs until she was squeezing his nipple.

"Hell yes, darling,"

She squeezed his other nipple, and they came together for a kiss. Their tongues twisted together faster now, her nerve endings tingling in response to the smell and taste of him on her.

"Should we go to the bedroom?" Nicole whispered in his ear.

"I don't know if I can stop long enough to move." He unbuttoned his pants, and she slid her hand down, gripping his manhood.

"Nicole," he moaned.

She leaned over him to pull the lamp chain for the light on the side table, and as she did so; he took her nipple in his mouth, lightly nibbling on it. Warmth flooded her. Her juices had long since soaked through her matching lace underwear. Her core ached with want. Once the light was off, she climbed off him, and he groaned. She knelt in front of him and pulled down his zipper. He helped her shimmy off his pants. As soon as those were out of the way she wrapped her hand around him, slowing moving up and down his cock.

Sean pushed himself further back in the loveseat and spread his legs to give her more access. Nicole looked up to see him watching the rise and fall of her breasts as she gripped him harder, needing to possess him. She sped up her movements. The corners of her mouth ticked up as she watched the furrowing of his brow and the way he was biting the inside of his cheek. She cupped his balls in her hand and began squeezing them gently. Then she took him into her mouth and breathed in the scent of him, mingled with the freshly showered scent of sandalwood and citrus. Her heart sang as he moaned his approval.

"Nicole, that feels so good. Yes, take all of me in." And she did. Then she pulled up and swirled her tongue on the top of his cock. She licked down the vein and then took his balls into her mouth. Sean wrapped his hand in her hair, carefully guiding her as she sucked. He bore down and started thrusting as she started going faster. The need pooled in her. She wanted him inside her now. She pulled back and looked up at him; his eyes were half-lidded. He was her pawn now. She sat next to him, took his hand and rubbed his finger against her clit. He got the message and began stroking her as she guided his hand. Then he slid a finger into her wet pussy.

"Yes, baby, right there. Oh yes, give me more," she panted.

He slowly pushed another finger in.

"God, you're so tight," he moaned. The desire in his voice just made her wetter. Her juices were coating his hand now, and she wanted him to keep going, but she needed his cock. He had one hand in her pussy and the other hand was kneading her ass, and she was on the brink of coming. She made herself move away, and then she put his hand on his cock. He began stroking himself.

"One sec," she gasped, and ran out of the room to the bedroom. She came back with coconut oil, vanilla-flavored lube, and condoms. She knelt, put lube in her hand and applied it to him, then she started sucking, sliding her mouth down the length of him.

"You're killing me, Nicole."

She tasted pre-cum in her mouth and knew neither of them could wait much longer. Reluctantly, she released him and opened the condom. Slowly she rolled it down over his rock-hard cock and then she climbed on top of him.

"Oh darling," he sighed as she took him in inch by inch until she was full. She paused for a moment.

Sean put his hand on her left breast and then her right and rubbed each nipple with his thumbs.

"I love you, Nicole. Every inch of you." He continued fondling her breasts, and she began moving up and down, faster and faster. She looked at him, his brown eyes dilated. Nicole threw back her head and rode him, enjoying the throbbing pulse of their rhythm. He moved his hands off her breasts and gripped her ass. She leaned forward, her breasts scraping on the hair of his chest, adding delicious friction to her swollen nipples. They were both panting now.

"Yes, oh yes, yes..." Sean moaned.

She sped up her movements, pushing faster and faster. He matched her stroke for stroke as they hit the top of that roller coaster, and then her thoughts disappeared in the avalanche of her orgasm.

She pulsed through delicious aftershocks, slowly rocking to a stop, and then she was limp on top of him. They stayed together. He rubbed his hands down her back until he was cupping her ass. She enjoyed the beat of his heart against her chest.

"I don't think I've ever been this content," she sighed.

He kissed the crown of her head in response.

They lay entwined for a while on the couch, then took turns in the shower. Once they were all ready for bed, they went to Nicole's bedroom. Soon they were cuddling under the comforter, content but not yet tired.

"You grew up here in Marley Creek, but your parents aren't in town, are they?" Sean asked as he traced Nicole's profile with his finger.

"No, they aren't. They moved to Orlando, gosh, about fourteen years ago, not too long after I started working at Ida B."

"Gotcha. Do they visit much?"

"I usually visit them during spring break. Sometimes they come to town for Thanksgiving or early summer. They never come back during the winter. They have become the kind of people who don't even own a winter coat at this point. Mostly we FaceTime. My parents love cruises. That's why they moved to Orlando. They wanted to be close to where cruise ships dock."

"I've never been on a cruise," Sean murmured as he ran a hand through her hair.

"I don't think you're missing anything."

Sean nuzzled her neck.

"Sean, I want to know all about you, your family, the first concert you went to, your first car. I want to know all the answers to the security questions you get asked to verify your identity online!" She laughed.

He chuckled and kissed the tip of her nose.

She continued. "What about your family? I know you said your parents are divorced. Did either of them get remarried?"

Sean stopped kissing Nicole's neck and moved slightly away from her. "Compared to your parents' relationship, my family is a tangled mess, and I'm thinking that is sugar-coating it. I don't really want to spend time we could be cuddling talking about my family."

Her face fell. "I'm sorry."

He put a finger up, "No, don't be sorry." He cupped her cheek. "You basically bared your soul to me. I can talk about things that broke me. I want to tell you." He rubbed his collarbone. It just still hurts, you know?"

She nodded and caressed his face.

"Right after the divorce, my dad got remarried. When I was in junior high, my mom got remarried."

"That must have been tough, remarriages during your pre-teen years. Do you have brothers and sisters?"

Sean held up a hand. His voice was flat. "By the time I graduated from high school, my dad was on marriage three, then while I was in college my mom caught up and was on marriage number three too And since then, my dad has gotten married and divorced a couple more times. My mom got divorced again. She finally realized marriage wasn't for her, and she's had a couple of long-term live-in boyfriends. I have so many step-siblings I need a family forest instead of a family tree to fit everyone in."

"Does it bother you? As an only child, anything involving brothers and sisters is completely foreign to me."

"Having an extended family so large I don't think they'd all fit in Jesse's Pub? No, that part doesn't bother me. I suppose it's kind of nice in its own way? The thing that gets to me is the casual way both my parents have been in and out of marriages collecting ex's and kids like some people collect beer steins."

"Maybe I've idealized the pre-divorce days of my childhood. Back then, I was the only child, and I felt loved. During the divorce, I felt pulled in different directions by both of them, like I was a prize and in my kid brain, it wasn't bad. Then by the time I was in high school, it was like I was their unpaid nanny. Both of them would want me to watch whatever younger kids were in the picture while they dated their newest fling. Of course, when your parents ask you to do stuff, you want to do it. You don't get cynical about their motives, right?"

Nicole nodded.

"It was a real mindfuck for me."

"Did you..." she started and stopped.

"Go on, you can ask me anything you want."

"I was wondering if you've tried therapy, but I didn't think it was really my business."

He took her hand. "Nicole, we are in this for the long haul as far as I am concerned."

She gave his hand a big squeeze. "I love you," she whispered. "I don't think I'll ever tire of saying that."

"Good," he said simply. "Yes, I did therapy back when I was in college, and it helped so much. It also helped me to clarify my thoughts on having kids."

Nicole held her breath. Her skin suddenly got clammy, and her pulse beat in her ears. She'd meant what she'd said about being willing to risk her heart with Sean, but apparently her body was not fully on board yet. "Oh?" she squeaked out.

"My therapist helped me to make peace with my resentment toward my parents and my step and half brothers and sisters. I realized what I wanted was a constant companion. Someone to share my life who wanted to share their life with me. I want us to be able to go on a trip at the drop of a hat, to only have to consider each other in our life plans. I want to live for the day every day and not always have one eye on the future."

"I like kids, don't get me wrong. They are delightful and sometimes are so much smarter than adults. I just don't want most of the best years I'll have to be focused on being responsible for the growth of another human into an adult. If you ask me, and you did, too many people on this planet don't give any thought to what raising a child means. Like they need to take classes."

"I'm sure you'd be a great dad." She acknowledged.

"Considering how little I want to be a dad, I don't know. I appreciate the vote of confidence, but it's not for me." He shrugged.

Nicole scooched over until they were lying face to face. She pushed her leg in between his and kissed him on his forehead, his cheeks, along his jawline, and then she came in for a kiss. She began with a chaste kiss, then tugged his bottom lip between her teeth. His tongue entered her mouth, and they were tasting each other again. Her hardened nipples were rubbing against his chest. The evidence of his arousal was pressing against her core.

She pulled back slightly and took his chin in her hand. "I'm ready to have adventures with you."

He leaned in and started kissing her like a starving man at a buffet. She leaned her head back, and he began kissing her neck while his hands roamed down seeking her warmth. Soon she was two fingers full, and he was swirling another finger around her clit. She moaned and he twisted so that he was on top of her. He reached over to grab another condom from the box, slipping it on and then adding a little lube to his fingers. He rubbed his lubed finger over her clit, then slipped it into her wet pussy, making sure she was ready before he entered her.

"Yes, oh my God, yes," she said. His thoughtfulness was as much of a turn-on as the way his fingers knew exactly where to press and stroke.

Chapter Thirty-One

A crick in his neck woke him up. He wasn't used to Nicole's bed or sharing a bed with her yet. He smiled. Best crick ever, as far as he was concerned. According to Nicole's vintage bedside clock, it wasn't even six o'clock. Sean knew he wouldn't be able to fall back asleep, as tempting as Nicole's bed was. He took a quick shower and then decided to wake up Nicole the only way he could—with the delicious smell of freshly ground coffee and breakfast cooking on the stove.

He walked into the kitchen and rummaged through the fridge, pantry, and cabinets quietly. A short time later, Sean found a bag of Jamaican Me Crazy Coffee from Books and Beans and a French press. In the refrigerator, he found half a dozen eggs, ham, and a few vegetables. He thought a Denver scramble would be the perfect breakfast for the two of them.

He ground the coffee beans and heated water, then he went to work chopping the veggies and ham and whisking the eggs. He added butter to Nicole's cast iron skillet, then sauteed the vegetables. Once they were soft, he added the egg and ham mixture on top, gently mixing everything together and scrambling it. Once the eggs were firm, he plated half for Nicole and the other half for himself. He grated a little cheddar cheese on top, then covered the dishes. He was trying to decide if bringing breakfast to Nicole in bed was a bit much when she walked into the kitchen.

He put down his spatula and enveloped her in a good morning hug.

She nuzzled his cheek and mumbled. "I need coffee."

He poured her a cup. "Do you take cream or sugar?"

"Just a splash of milk." He added milk from the carton that was already on the counter from making the scramble and handed her a mug of coffee.

Her auburn hair was mussed from the night before, and the oversized T-shirt she wore barely covered her round bottom. She took a drink of the coffee, and he copped a feel. She set down her mug and wrapped her arms around his neck. He leaned in and gave her a kiss.

"You look beautiful in the morning."

"Thank you." She blushed. "You look amazing cooking in my kitchen."

Sean smiled broadly, his dimples popping. "I could get used to this."

"How soon do you have to go to Jesse's?"

"Did I tell you I hired a new sous chef?"

Nicole shook her head.

"His name is Lucas. We've been training all week and today, he's taking the lead. I need to head over at eight o'clock."

"Any chance you can call off?" Nicole rubbed herself against him like she was a cat, and he was a spot of sunshine. "Oh wait, I promised Devin and Zaina I'd do brunch with them at noon at your place."

He gave her a soft kiss.

"I'd say it's too soon for me to leave everything in Lucas's hands. How about I make you dinner tonight and include a side of this?" He fanned his arm down his side.

"I'm a very lucky girl." She batted her eyes at him.

"Yes, you are, and a good girl, too."

Nicole snorted and did a coffee spit take.

"Behold the effect I have on women. I stun them."

Nicole wiped her mouth and the tears of laughter from her eyes. She cleared her throat and then said, "I didn't think anything could top last night, but here we are."

He reached over and held her hand. "Darling, there's plenty more where that came from."

"Did you mean this breakfast or last night?"

"How about both?"

"Both are really good," Nicole said.

They ate in a peaceful silence, broken a few times with laughter and plans for later that evening. Sean would go into Jesse's soon. He was pleased that he'd get to see her while he worked today. He'd leave Jesse's early and let Lucas finish out the day so he could go home, feed Hermie, and grab a change of clothes and his toiletries bag. Then he'd stop by the market and pick up groceries for dinner, then meet her back at her house by seven.

Sean glanced at his phone, and his heart sank. His workday was almost at hand, and he wasn't ready to leave Nicole. "Would you like me to tuck you into bed?" he offered.

"Yes, I would. I'd love it so much. I'd pull you right down onto the bed with me and I wouldn't let you go to work." She came around the table, put her arms around his neck and whispered into his ear, "I'd wrap my legs around you and then I'd flip us over, slide down you and take all of that beautiful cock of yours into my mouth, licking and sucking you."

Sean groaned and adjusted his pants. "Woman, what are you doing to me?" She pressed a kiss to the crown of his head and then walked away to get a sweater from the front closet. Swaying her hips as she walked, she stopped to turn and catch him ogling her. After he collected himself, he started clearing the table. Nicole joined him in putting the dishes into the dishwasher.

Warmth spread through his chest as he placed the silverware in the dishwasher. He couldn't help himself from humming a little as they worked. After years on his own, he was home. She felt like his home more than his actual home and family did.

He wanted to stay and hang out with Nicole all day, but it was time to leave. Nicole walked him to the door where he gave her a kiss that curled both their toes. "I'll see you soon," he said, his husky voice filled with promises.

She gazed at him, her eyes slowly focusing. She blinked languidly. "Love you."

He smiled and walked to his Jeep. When he got in and started the engine, he looked up and she waved goodbye. He returned the wave and then backed out of the driveway and went to work.

Chapter Thirty-Two

Nicole watched Sean pull out of her driveway, and then closed the door and flopped down in her recliner. She was a little achy from the night before, but it was a good ache. So many days over the last few years had been spent dealing with aches and pains in the aftermath of treatment, and it had been awful. But these aches were different. She pushed out the footrest and curled up. The sun shining on the chair had warmed it up, and she nestled down into it feeling like a very satisfied cat. She was well-fed, and better yet, she was well-loved. She pulled the throw off the loveseat and covered herself. Even though she'd just had coffee with Sean, within minutes she was fast asleep.

It was just after eleven o'clock when she woke up, feeling rested and ready for a tasty brunch. She treated herself to a nice long shower and used all her favorite gels and lotions as she got ready to meet the girls. Nicole took out the expensive satin bodysuit lingerie she'd bought and never gotten around to wearing years ago. She put it on under a soft, long sweater with leggings. Then she fluffed the ends of her hair, threw on some lip gloss and mascara, and she was good to go.

Nicole walked out into the sunshine and took a deep breath. The sun warmed her face, countering the chilly wind blowing from the north. She shivered for a moment and then put on a crochet hat from Zaina's shop. The events of the last twenty-four hours had her smiling widely with a sparkle in her eyes as she walked toward Jesse's Pub. For the first time in years, she'd have someone to share the holidays with this year. She wondered if Sean could take off any time over the holidays. She had promised to go on a short cruise with her parents for Christmas, and she'd already gotten the ticket. Unlike when she'd been with Duncan, she felt light as a feather as she thought about how the conversation would go with Sean. Knowing Sean, she was sure not only would he be happy to go with her, but he'd even enjoy her parents' company.

As she crossed the parking lot, she saw Zaina sitting in her car. She had her phone in her hand, and she was frowning. As Nicole got closer, she could see Zaina's face was pale. She stood in front of Zaina's car and now made eye contact with Zaina and pantomimed, "Are you okay?"

Zaina shook her head.

Nicole started walking around to Zaina's passenger door. She could hear a man's voice and she thought it was probably Mike, but she wasn't sure.

Zaina waved her off though, so Nicole gestured that she'd see Zaina inside.

Nicole walked into Jesse's Pub and looked around for Devin. She quickly found her sitting at a table near the fireplace. Nicole sat down across from Devin. She was momentarily speechless as she recalled the last time they'd gone to brunch.

"Something wrong?" Devin's eyebrows knit together.

Nicole propped up her chin on her palm. "I can't believe what a difference a few weeks can make. Absolutely nothing is wrong. I feel like a different person."

"You look like a different person!" Devin commented. Nicole sat up straighter in her seat, and Devin grabbed her hand. "I mean that in the best of ways, I swear you look like you just had a facial and a deep tissue massage."

Nicole waggled her eyebrows and said, "Well..."

Devin nodded her head, "I think we all really underestimate the health benefits of some good sex." She squinted, leaned in, and scrutinized Nicole's face. "Is that love I see?"

A red flush climbed up Nicole's neck, and she lowered her voice in answer, "Devin, he said I love you!"

Devin got up and went around the table to hug a sitting Nicole. "I'm so happy! You deserve so much love."

Nicole hugged her back awkwardly, "Dev."

"Yes, Nic?"

"Um, can you let go now? You know how I feel about too much PDA."

Devin gave her one more little squeeze and sat back down. "My bad, sorry about that."

"No worries, I'm over the moon right now. I'm surprised I can sit in the chair. I feel like I'm about to float away."

Devin raised a finger, and a server came over, "Can we get a pitcher of mimosas?"

The server nodded and brought over two champagne flutes and a pitcher of mimosas.

"We'll need one more glass," Devin said, and then turned to Nicole. "Where is Zaina?"

The server put another glass on the table. Nicole waited until he walked away before she spoke to her friend. "She was in her car on the phone when I was walking in. I was going to wait for her, but she gestured for me to come in. She looked upset Dev, I think she was talking to Mike."

Devin sighed and shook her head, "I hate to say it Nic, but I wish she would dump his ass. I don't trust him. I never have."

Nicole poured mimosas into each of the three glasses. "I know! I feel the same way. I don't know why she puts up with him."

"Who knows? I wonder though, if maybe she's looking for the fairytale. She had it pretty rough growing up. Her dad was never in the picture. She told me that until her mom met Mark, she'd never seen her mom date anyone. I think she'd say she's just trying to manifest Mr. Right."

"Pretty sure Mike is a manifestation of Mr. Wrong," Nicole quipped.

"Dang, Nic, tell me how you really feel." Zaina plopped into the seat next to Devin.

"Oh my God, I'm an asshole," Nicole said, smacking herself on the forehead.

Zaina slumped down in her seat and crossed her arms. "No, no, it's alright. It turns out you were right; that was him on the phone."

Devin scooted her chair over and wrapped an arm around Zaina. "What happened, Z?"

Zaina sighed shakily, tears filling her eyes. "He said," she paused and took a breath, and then sobbed quietly, "He said..."

"Go on Hon, you can tell us," Devin said in the voice she used to calm the twins down.

Nicole pushed a mimosa flute in front of her friend.

Zaina took her napkin, unrolled it, and used it to blot her eyes. She pursed her lips. "He said," she swallowed, "that he fell out of love. That he'd met someone else."

"That fucker." Nicole mumbled. "What a dick."

Zaina started nodding her head, "Yes, yes, what a dick." She hit the table with her fist. "I wasted two years with that, that putz!"

"Let it out, Z," Devin continued rubbing her back.

"Do you have any idea how much I gave up for him?"

They both shook their heads no.

"Let me tell you. He didn't like me running, said it made me too lean. Who does that? So, I stopped running. He said he loved my hair and I shouldn't change it. So, I haven't done anything different with my hair in years. He said his phone calls should always come first, so I've stayed home at night instead of going to networking events, or local witch meet-ups, or just hanging out with you girls. All for what?"

"Bupkis." Nicole said.

"Bupkis?" Zaina asked.

"Yes, my grandpa used to say that all the time. Bupkis, it means like nothing. If you have bupkis, you have like less than a crumb."

"Got it. Yes, exactly! I got bupkis for all the time I spent trying to fit into Mike's tiny box of acceptable behaviors."

"Not anymore." Devin held up her glass.

Zaina sniffed the last of her tears and raised her glass. "Not anymore," she nodded.

Nicole smiled, "Here's to not anymore."

They clinked their glasses, and all took a long drink.

Zaina set down her glass and looked at Nicole. "You look ridiculously happy. I'm sorry to come in and be a big old bummer when we should be celebrating you."

Nicole waved her hand. "No problem. I feel so happy, I'm almost bulletproof." Zaina gave Nicole's hand a big squeeze.

"You know what's going to happen now?" Devin asked dryly.

"No, what?" Zaina's eyes widened.

"Nicole and her new man are going to get you coupled up so they can double date with you and your future man."

"Hey!" Nicole crossed her arms, "I'm not in the match-making business."

Zaina shook her head, "I think I'm in the no-man-for-a-while business."

"Mm-hmm," Devin said, and she stood up. "Let's get some food. I'm starving."

"This time I'm getting some of the Nutella French toast. Zaina, you have to try some too. Devin said it's life-changing."

"I tell you what, it really is."

"Lead the way." Zaina held her arm out, and Devin started walking to the buffet.

Nicole glanced over at the omelet station, and Sean wasn't there. He must be in the back. She wanted to see him, but she also didn't want to call attention to their relationship in his place of work.

They filled their plates with plenty of Nutella French toast as well as deviled eggs, thick slices of bacon and little yogurt parfaits. By the time their plates were cleared away, the pitcher was gone, and they'd had more laughs than tears as Nicole shared some highlights of her weekend. Even Zaina was in good spirits for most of the meal.

Devin's phone pinged. She looked down at it. "Ladies, it looks like my time is up. Ben is calling for reinforcements."

They stood up and began making their way out of the restaurant. When they got to the hostess stand, a voice said, "Nicole."

Nicole grinned and turned around into Sean's embrace. She gave him a warm squeeze. "You look so hot in your chef's whites." She spoke low for only him to hear. "I can't wait to get you out of them tonight." She moved away from him, and he put his arm around her waist and kissed the crown of her head.

"Ladies, thanks for coming to Jesse's Pub today. I hope everything was amazing."

"So good." Zaina said, patting her flat stomach.

"Excellent as always, Chef," Devin said.

Nicole touched her cheeks; she was thinking if she kept smiling this much, her face was going to hurt. *More good aches* she thought.

She moved so that she was just holding his hand now. "See you about seven?" she confirmed.

"I'll come loaded with groceries to make you a Michelin Star dinner."

"And a side of prime beef right here, all for me." She gave him a pat on his chest.

Zaina guffawed.

He rolled his eyes. "Maybe leave the food puns to me?"

"We'll see about that, baby," she teased.

"Behave," he said with a wink and kissed her cheek. "Bye for now." He turned and began walking back toward the kitchen.

On each side of her, Devin and Zaina were fanning themselves dramatically.

"So hot," Zaina said as the doors swung shut behind Sean.

"He is a fine-looking man."

"And he's all mine."

Epilogue

Nicole turned off her monitor and pushed back from her desk. The first day back after Spring Break was in the books, and she was ready for another vacation. She picked up her purse and looked out the window for Sean's Jeep.

Nancy spoke up from the copy machine. "Is your honey coming to pick you up today?"

Nicole turned from the window, smiling widely, her ponytail swishing. "Yep, we're going over to Marley Lake Park."

"You both are just too cute. The weather is perfect for going to the lake. I'm so glad it warmed up after last week."

"Me too. We had nothing but rain and cold around here all of Spring Break."

Nancy leaned over and looked out the window. "Your knight in shining armor is here." Nancy quickly walked outside and began chatting it up with Sean.

Nicole ran outside to save Sean from Nancy's probing questions.

"Sean, can I ask if you've ever been engaged?"

Sean shoved his hands into his pockets. "Well, I uh, can't..."

Nicole's face burned red hot, and she loudly interrupted, "Nancy, I think I heard Mr. Steve was looking for you. Something about ordering more Super-Sorb?"

Nancy turned away from Sean. "Alright, alright, I'll be there in a second," she grumbled.

As soon as Nancy was back inside, Nicole took Sean's hand and started pulling him toward his Jeep. "We'd better get out of here before she comes back."

"I take it Mr. Steve wasn't looking for her?"

"Nope."

Sean laughed and Nicole joined him, and they drove out of the parking lot heading toward Marley Lake.

"I was tempted to take the top off, but I thought the wind might be a little too cold for you."

"Aww, thank you, baby." Nicole placed her hand on Sean's knee.

Given the unseasonably warm day, the park was full of kids, some of whom Nicole recognized, sliding down the slides and climbing on the jungle gym. The benches surrounding the playground were filled with parents, grandparents, and babysitters. Nicole held Sean's hand as they walked past the kids and their parents. There had been a time when seeing carefree kids with their moms had made her sad, but today she felt a warmth in her chest, knowing she had Sean. She put her hand in her jeans pocket to make sure the little box she carried was still there.

Once they were away from the shouts of the kids, Sean found a level spot and put down their picnic basket. He pulled out the buffalo-plaid blanket stored inside and began spreading it out. Nicole took an end and helped. "If you had told me last fall that I was going to be the kind of person who not only owned a picnic basket but used it for picnics, I would have thought you were crazy."

Sean patted the ground, and Nicole sat down beside him. She leaned in and kissed him. She slowly let it deepen, gently pushing his mouth open with her tongue. As they kissed, he wrapped an arm around her, bringing her closer to him. She pulled back from his kiss and lightly kissed his neck. As she kissed him, he pulled her onto his lap. She wrapped her legs around him and felt the hard length of him rubbing against the seam of her jeans. She stopped kissing and looked around.

"Maybe we should have picnicked in my backyard?"

Sean chuckled against her neck. "I picked this spot because of the bushes. No one can see us."

"Thank goodness." Nicole said and began kissing Sean again. The raspy hair of his stubble made her lips extra sensitive, and she relished the feeling as she brought her lips back to his mouth.

They kissed for a while longer. A gentle breeze feathered the hair on Sean's head, and the twittering of birds nearby combined to make Nicole's heart ready to burst. Sean rested his forehead against Nicole's.

"We should eat. I'm working on a couple of new recipes, and I thought I'd try them on you."

Nicole was suddenly famished. "Now that you mention it, I only had a bag of baked potato chips at lunch."

Sean shook his head, "I've failed as a chef boyfriend." He frowned dramatically.

"You're the best chef boyfriend, and I am sure I'll be reminded of that when I eat whatever deliciousness you've made for us!"

Nicole got off Sean's lap. Sean opened the basket and handed plates, plastic ware, and glasses to Nicole.

"You brought champagne flutes? How fancy!"

"To be fair, they are plastic."

"True. Well then, semi-fancy."

Sean pulled out three plastic containers, took the tops off, and began making plates for Nicole and himself. "I'm working on ideas for May. We'll have Mother's Day, graduations, first communions, and of course, our regular weekend brunches. So, I've been working on this new tarragon chicken salad. I'm thinking of using my buttermilk-brined chicken and then adding finely chopped fennel and purple onion, a little mayo and a little tarragon. I also have pimento cheese potato salad, and then for a side, dilly beans. It's a play on traditional Southern dishes. I'm thinking of trying out chess pie tartlets too, but we'll see."

Nicole took the offered plate, and soon her mouth and tummy were full. "Everything is delicious, Sean! I'm sure everyone coming into Jesse's Pub will leave full and happy. And speaking of happy..." She turned to Sean, who had finished his lunch and was packing up the rest of their meal, leaving out the champagne glasses.

She pulled the small red box out of her pocket and offered it. Suddenly she felt unsure. Sweat broke out on her back, and her voice shook a little as she spoke. "Sean, for the last six months you have practically lived at my house. During all that time, you never pushed me to give you your own part of the closet or asked me to make room in my garage so you could park the Jeep in there. You certainly never asked me to give you a key. Even after Ethan came to stay in your tiny place, you didn't push me to consider living together. One of the many reasons I love you is because you are easy-going but you aren't a pushover. I would hate that. You are a strong person, and that allows you to give me space." Her face was red now. Declarations of love were not her strong suit.

"Here." She handed him the box.

He took the box and opened it. A big smile spread across his face, showing off his dimples. Nicole traced a dimple with her finger and then he gave her a hug.

"I love it." He pulled out his key ring and added the house key.

"I love you, baby." Nicole said and gave him a kiss. He was sitting on the blanket and Nicole lay down, putting her head in his lap. She shivered when he took out her hair tie and combed his hand through her hair.

"Before I met you, I was concerned with one thing and one thing only, making sure my restaurant was successful. I literally ate, slept, and dreamed about Jesse's Pub. Then you came along and dumped your egg white omelet on the ground."

"Hey, I didn't drop it on purpose!"

He ignored her and continued. "And I got so lucky because you didn't get stuck in your answer of no. You thought it over and took a second chance on the smallest thing, allowing yourself to enjoy a delicious meal. Then you took a second chance on a date with me. Later, I got to be the one to give us a second chance. You showed me how much I meant to you when you opened up and shared all of yourself with me. Knowing you and having you in my life has changed everything for me. You are my partner, you are my family, you are the only one I need in this life."

A lump formed in Nicole's throat, and her hands were shaking slightly in anticipation. Was he going to do what she thought he was going to do? She sat up on the blanket; sweat was dripping down her back now.

He pulled out a small bag from the basket and shook out the velvet box.

Nicole's mouth dropped open.

Sean stood up, got down on one knee, and opened the jewelry box. "Nicole, you are the best person I know, and I want to spend the rest of my life making you smile. Will you marry me?"

Tears spilled down Nicole's face, and she was momentarily unable to speak. She nodded her head vigorously, and then she threw her arms around Sean, almost knocking him off balance.

"Yes, you don't have to ask me twice! I will marry you!"

Sean kissed the top of her head and then took her hand in his and slid the bezel-set engagement ring on her finger. "I'm not gonna lie. I was a little worried you might turn me down the first time I asked."

"Really?"

Sean held his thumb and forefinger a few millimeters apart.

Nicole put her face in her hands. "Ugh, I feel terrible."

"Don't! Don't feel bad at all! Asking you to marry me should be a little scary! This is it for me. You're my one and only."

Tears were filling Nicole's eyes, her cheeks flushed. "I love you so much."

Sean cocked his head to the side, a twinkle in his eyes as he said, "Darling, you make me a cheddar man."

Nicole groaned. "Am I in for a lifetime of food puns?"

Sean nodded gravely and gave her a quick kiss.

Nicole sighed dramatically, then paused before saying, "It's just as well. I'm no gouda without you."

***

If you loved Sean and Nicole, come back to Marley Creek for Jasper and Zaina's story https://a.co/d/3iKQ4BM